SOLAY

Also by Mark Jonathan Harris

———

Come the Morning
Confessions of a Prime-Time Kid
The Last Run
With a Wave of the Wand

SOLAY

MARK JONATHAN HARRIS

BRADBURY PRESS • NEW YORK

Maxwell Macmillan Canada • Toronto
Maxwell Macmillan International
New York • Oxford • Singapore • Sydney

Bradbury Press
Macmillan Publishing Company
866 Third Avenue
New York, NY 10022

Maxwell Macmillan Canada, Inc.
1200 Eglinton Avenue East
Suite 200
Don Mills, Ontario M3C 3N1

Macmillan Publishing Company is part of the Maxwell Communication Group of Companies.

First edition
Printed and bound in the United States of America
10   9   8   7   6   5   4   3   2   1

The text of this book is set in Caledonia.

LIBRARY OF CONGRESS CATALOGING-IN-PUBLICATION DATA
Harris, Mark Jonathan, date.
Solay / Mark Jonathan Harris. — 1st ed.
p.   cm.
Summary: Unhappy in her new school where she is the favorite target of bullies, ten-year-old Melissa finds comfort and gains self-confidence through her relationship with a visitor from another planet.
ISBN 0-02-742655-6
[1. Extraterrestrial beings—Fiction.   2. Self-confidence—Fiction.   3. Bullies—Fiction.   4. Schools—Fiction.   5. Moving, Household—Fiction.]   I. Title.
PZ7.H24229So   1993
[Fic]—dc20   92-33012

For Zoltan Gross,
who showed me how to find Zironia

For Melissa Ballard, the music of Bach, Brahms, and Chopin all made her stomach curdle. They were the composers her father listened to each morning to calm him through the traffic on the way to Ralph Waldo Emerson Elementary.

Today he put one of his favorite Bach cassettes into the tape deck—the *Brandenburg* Concertos—and waved the musicians onward with his forefinger, steering the Volvo with his other hand. Melissa sat in the front seat beside him, her stomach churning to the music as she rolled and unrolled the cuffs of her new jeans. No matter how she fixed them, they didn't look right.

She looked out the window at the other cars on

Mimosa Boulevard. She was sure the parents driving them were listening to news or sports, or that their children were turning the dial to catch the latest rock or rap hit. No other father in Crestwood Estates could possibly be conducting the air with his finger or loudly humming Bach. Melissa kept her window closed so any classmates who passed them wouldn't think her any nerdier than they already did.

The Ballards had moved to California that August, and Melissa had started Emerson in September. Now it was November, and though she had tried hard to become a part of her new school, her classmates hadn't been very welcoming. From the first day they had treated her with suspicion—as if she had arrived from another planet instead of New York City. She had done her best to wear the right clothes, to laugh at the right jokes, to watch the right TV programs (although that was pretty hard when you were only allowed seven hours of TV a week). None of it helped. Her teacher, Mrs. Rademacher, hadn't made Melissa's September any easier when she held her up to the class as an "example of what a person can accomplish if one sets one's sights high enough."

"If she looks up all the time, guess what she might step in," Caitlin Perry had whispered to Rochelle Kaminsky, loud enough for almost everyone but Mrs. Rademacher to hear.

As Mr. Ballard turned down School Lane, Melissa

recalled the awful weeks of being trailed by fifth graders holding their noses and pointing to her shoes.

It was too bad people couldn't be like buildings, she thought glumly, staring at a group of one-story stucco buildings painted the same desert pastel colors as the other houses in the area. The school, the fire station, even the McDonald's in Crestwood Estates, were all carefully designed and painted to blend in with the rest of the community.

While Mr. Ballard led the musicians to the close of the Fourth Concerto, Melissa rolled up her right jeans cuff one more time. Now it looked shorter than her left.

Mr. Ballard stopped Melissa's hand before she could reroll her pants again. "Don't worry about your jeans. Despite what the ads say, clothes don't make the person." He tapped his forehead. "Brains do. Now run off and light up the classroom."

Melissa felt more like vanishing into a black hole.

Awaiting her on the lawn by the school's front entrance were the fifth-grade Fashion Critics. Caitlin was dressed in pink today, Celia in green, and Rochelle in blue and gold. Like models in a magazine, they were all perfectly pressed, color-coordinated, and accessorized.

Melissa's only escape was through the school yard and behind the main building to Mrs. Rademacher's classroom. But directly in her path, playing kickball, were two of her least favorite classmates—David Nishikawa and Dougie Drollinger—the smartest boy and the dumbest in Mrs. Rademacher's class.

Melissa chose to brave the Critics.

"Oh, she's bought a new pair of jeans."

"At least they're not from Kmart."

"But look at those cuffs." The girls started to giggle.

Melissa resisted the impulse to look down. With her eyes focused firmly on the doorway, she passed by the girls, shredding their clothes in her mind, leaving them in rags and tatters.

"Hey, Miss Head-in-the-Clouds, cuffs are gross in tight jeans!" Celia called after her.

Melissa's stomach tightened and she could taste her breakfast in her mouth. She'd messed up once again.

She didn't know why she kept on trying.

Mrs. Rademacher led off each day with mathematics because, she said, the discipline and order of numbers were the best way to warm up the mind. This morning she began the lesson by handing back the tests of the day before.

Mrs. Rademacher always made a show of returning marked papers and saved for last the top five. Melissa felt her stomach begin to flutter.

A large woman, Mrs. Rademacher shuffled slowly up and down the rows of desks, listing from side to side like someone balancing on a rocky boat. The more papers she returned, the queasier Melissa felt. But when it came to the final five, hers, as usual, was among them. Melissa glanced two rows over at David Nishikawa. In his lap, David uncapped a small bottle of Tums and slipped a tablet into his mouth.

"And with ninety-seven percent, Caitlin Perry," Mrs. Rademacher announced. She looked over the top of her half-frame reading glasses. "Excellent work, Caitlin."

Caitlin took her exam as if she expected no less. "That's a pretty shawl you're wearing today," she gushed to the teacher.

The next paper Mrs. Rademacher handed back was Celia Lewis's—also a 97. Celia was Caitlin's best friend and constant shadow. Whatever Caitlin did, Celia tried to imitate. Melissa sometimes wondered what would happen if Caitlin flunked a test. Would Celia do the same?

Now only three people were without their tests: Melissa and David and Sally Gillkey.

Mrs. Rademacher walked over to Sally, who wasn't usually among the top five, and returned her paper. Sally's 98, she noted, should be an inspiration to the class, an example of what they all could accomplish if only they applied themselves.

"If I sat behind David I could get a ninety-eight, too," grumbled Rochelle in a loud whisper. From the red marks Melissa could see on her test, it looked as if Rochelle had more wrong answers than right.

Mrs. Rademacher leveled one of her very disappointed looks in Rochelle's direction. "None of us likes to do less than we are capable of," she admonished, lowering her glasses further down her nose. "But resentment is not the answer to disappointment. The answer is to work to our capacities."

Rochelle faked regret and stared at her nails. They were painted alternately blue and gold today to match her skirt and shirt.

"And now"—Mrs. Rademacher beamed approval—"continuing to maintain the high standards he has set for himself, David Nishikawa. Well done, David, a one hundred percent."

David accepted his exam with a slight nod of his head and glanced nervously at Melissa.

"And, finally, with one hundred percent, plus the extra-credit problem—the top grade in the class—our newcomer from New York City. Congratulations, Melissa, you're setting new standards of excellence for us all."

Melissa took back her test and carefully folded it. From the corner of her eye, she saw David twist the Tums bottle in his lap as if he were choking it. A few seats in front of her, Caitlin and Celia leaned across the aisle to whisper to each other. And at the other end of the room, Dougie Drollinger raised the corner of his mouth in a sneer.

Melissa put the test into her notebook without looking at it. She was sorry now that she'd solved the extra-credit problem. The satisfaction wasn't worth the price she knew she'd have to pay for it.

At noon, Melissa took her lunchbox and a book from her locker and walked to the bench at the far corner of the playground, where she usually ate alone. She liked the spot because it was far enough away so that people didn't hassle her, but close enough that she could watch what was happening on the playground.

She set her lunchbox on the wooden bench and opened it. The sandwiches her mother always sealed in plastic bags were unwrapped. Gingerly, Melissa lifted one corner of the whole-wheat bread. A wad of chewing gum was mixed in with the tuna fish. She put the sandwiches on the bench and stared at the rest of her lunch: an apple with two big bites in one side, the wrapper from the missing chocolate cake, and an orange juice can that rattled when Melissa picked it up.

"What's the matter, Miss Perfect? Don't you like the lunch your momma made you?"

Melissa looked up to see Dougie Drollinger and David Nishikawa watching her with glee. Even from fifteen yards away, she could see the chocolate icing on Dougie's jeering lips.

"Does your lunch set new standards?" David asked with a triumphant grin.

Too discouraged to reply, Melissa turned her back to them and walked over to the trash can. As she dumped out the spoiled food, the three Fashion Critics wandered by. "Did something spoil your lunch?" Caitlin asked, pretending concern.

"You could share ours." Celia held out an apple core.

Melissa snapped her lunchbox shut and started to walk away.

"I bet Miss Extra Credit's going to be hungry this afternoon," Dougie crowed.

"I bet she is," David said, though his grin had already faded. Melissa wondered if he was disappointed that she wasn't crying.

Across the field, she spotted Mr. Gunderson, the sixth-grade teacher, patrolling the yard. She headed in his direction, knowing that the boys wouldn't follow.

"Better not tell," Dougie warned.

"Wipe your mouth," David told him, rubbing his own with the back of his hand.

But Melissa knew better than to tell on them. Why cause more grief?

She stared back at them a moment, wishing that the ground might open and swallow them up, but no earthquake struck to grant her wish. Left on her own, she could only escape to the lavatory to hide out until class resumed.

Twilight was Melissa's favorite time of the day. In the evenings, she would climb the grassy hill behind her house, plunk down underneath the gnarled oak tree at the top, and watch the sun disappear behind the ridges of Crestwood Estates. The peacefulness of the hilltop, the changing colors of the clouds and sky, always cheered her.

This evening she sat, as usual, beneath the oak, letting the bad memories of her day fade with the colors of the sky. In the twilight, she noticed low over the horizon a peculiar amber-red light. The light glowed an instant like a red-hot coal, then shot across the dusky sky. As it whizzed overhead, Melissa saw the beam was coming from the top of a long, silvery object. A plane? A rocket ship? A shooting star? The strange missile hovered a moment over the next hill, then rose straight up into the air and disappeared in a bank of clouds.

Melissa rose, brushed the dirt and leaves from the seat of her new jeans, and scanned the darkening sky once more. Probably a trick of light, she thought; the sun's rays reflecting from a balloon or an airplane, or maybe even a meteor—although meteors fell; they didn't shoot straight up, did they? She wondered if anyone else had seen it.

She looked down at the evenly spaced houses, the fenced yards, and the spacious streets of her neighborhood. *Not just better places to live, but a better life*, the real-estate brochure had promised. The street-lamps were just turning on, illuminating the few people on the windy sidewalks. None of them was looking skyward. In the streets, no drivers had stopped their cars to gaze at the heavens.

Melissa checked her digital watch: 5:27. Her mother should be returning from her downtown office very soon now. Her car was probably among the stream of headlights turning onto Autumn Glen Road. At the bottom of the hill, Melissa could see her father silhouetted against the warm yellow light of their kitchen. Wednesday was their housekeeper's day off— her father's night to cook—but once again he was heating up some take-out food he'd picked up on his way home from the university. In the windows of other homes, Melissa could see children setting the table or sprawled in front of TV sets.

The wind picked up now, rustling the branches above her. Or was it something else? Her heart pounding, Melissa leaned against the oak tree and looked cautiously upward.

Whoooooeeeee!

The high-pitched cry trailed a large white object that floated to the ground as softly as a beach ball. Only it wasn't a ball. Uncurled and stretched, the object appeared to be a creature with thick arms and legs and about Melissa's height. It was dressed in a white jumpsuit and what looked like an oversized motorcycle helmet. The helmet was attached to the clothes, like a hooded ski jacket. Or a space suit.

This can't be, Melissa thought to herself.

"Can't be what?" a birdlike voice chirped from behind the helmet.

"Really happening," Melissa said aloud in surprise. She gave her arm a sharp pinch to be sure she wasn't dreaming.

The white-suited figure didn't disappear. "Is that a new way to greet people?" the stranger spoke again in its high-pitched voice. "It wasn't on the tapes I studied."

Melissa pinched herself a second time.

"Hello to you, too." The visitor raised a gloved hand

and mimicked Melissa's gesture. Then it touched a button on the side of its helmet, and the plastic visor lowered like an electric window. Inside the huge helmet was a tiny, round face, as white as a clown's, with wide-set eyes and a small, turned-up nose.

The nose twitched like a rabbit's, then let out a loud sneeze. "Phoosh! Your air is even dirtier than they said. I hope I'm not allergic."

The visitor unzipped its helmet. Underneath the bulky spacesuit, the stranger was no bigger than Melissa. But its skin was so white, it seemed almost bloodless. Making it look even paler, its black hair stood up straight on its head like freshly cut grass. The wide-set eyes were different colors—one pale blue, the other a coppery brown—like a Siberian husky's. A metallic blue ring adorned one round ear and a copper earring the other.

Melissa wondered if the creature was male or female.

"Do I look like a boy to you?" the intruder said.

Melissa jumped. "You did it again!" she exclaimed.

"Did what?" The stranger's wide forehead wrinkled in what Melissa took to be puzzlement, but then she wasn't very used to interpreting the expressions of space travelers . . . if that's what she really was.

"You read my mind," Melissa said.

"You asked a question. I answered."

"But I didn't ask it aloud."

"Thoughts speak just as loud as words."

I don't believe this, Melissa thought.

The girl shrugged her padded shoulders as if she couldn't care less what Melissa believed. "Is this Central Park?" she asked.

"Central Park!"

"Right. I'm looking for Fifth Avenue. Rockefeller Center."

"This isn't New York!" Melissa said in astonishment. "It's California."

The girl groaned. "My father always messes up these landings."

She studied the community below her. No dazzling glass and steel skyscrapers. Only tile roofs and stucco houses.

"How do I get to New York?" she asked.

"It's three thousand miles away," Melissa said.

The girl slapped her helmet against her leg. "*Magi, mugi, mungi!*" she exclaimed in what Melissa guessed was her own language. She wondered if the spacegirl were swearing.

"Well, wouldn't you swear if you ended up three thousand miles from where you were supposed to?"

"I don't swear," Melissa answered.

The spacegirl stared at her with her clashing eyes as if Melissa were the one who was peculiar. Then she surveyed the row of almost identical two-story houses on Melissa's street. "What kind of place is this?" she grumbled.

"It's a planned community."

"A very dull plan if you ask me."

"You're right," Melissa agreed.

But the girl turned and started down the hill with a lilt that suggested that Earth's gravity had as little impact on her as did Melissa.

Melissa sensed she was losing a great opportunity. "Wait!" she called, and hurried after her. "Where are you going?"

The girl shook her head. "Is everyone as slow as you are?"

"Slow?" Melissa smarted. "I just happen to be the brightest girl in my class."

"*Magi!*" the girl exclaimed again. "New York has to be more advanced than this." She continued gliding toward the houses below.

"I'm *from* New York," Melissa said, huffing. Although she was slightly taller, she had to take two steps for every one of the creature's to keep up.

"Really?" The girl stopped.

"I lived a few blocks from Central Park, on East Seventy-eighth Street."

"Then what are you doing here?"

"My father got a new job and we had to move."

"What a mistake!"

"I know." Melissa sighed.

They both glanced again at the community below. The houses of Crestwood Estates were laid out as symmetrically as the stakes in the fences that enclosed

14

them. As the wind swept through the empty back-yards, it rattled the lawn furniture and barbecues in nearly every lot.

"You should have refused to come," the girl declared. "You should have lain down on the ground and kicked and screamed and swore until your parents changed their minds."

"I didn't know it was going to be this bad," Melissa explained. "In New York I had friends. Here nobody likes me." She suddenly felt embarrassed to be telling all this to a stranger. She didn't even know where the girl was from.

"Zironia."

"Zironia?" Melissa asked.

"That's the planet where I come from," the spacegirl said impatiently.

"Well, what are *you* doing here?"

"I told you before. My father messed up. But I'm not going to sit around feeling sorry for myself about it. I'm going to New York," she announced, and started tromping through the field again.

"And just how are you going to do that?" Melissa followed after her.

"Watch and you'll see. We Zironians are very resourceful people. You could learn a lot from us."

The girl was as stuck-up as her nose, Melissa thought.

"My nose happens to be just the right angle for

people on my planet," she announced testily.

"Then everyone on your planet must be very rude," Melissa retorted.

The girl's wide brow crinkled again. "Rude?"

"Having no manners," Melissa explained.

"What are manners?" the girl asked.

"Maybe your planet's not as advanced as you think," Melissa couldn't resist saying. "Manners," she straightened her back and recited, "are the polite or proper way to treat other people. For instance, it's not polite to read other people's thoughts."

The stranger lifted her head haughtily. "Well if you don't want people to know your thoughts, you shouldn't think them."

This was too much. Melissa had never met anyone like this . . . this creature, who didn't follow any of the rules she'd been taught. It was confusing and exasperating and just a little bit exciting.

What was she going to do about it?

"You don't need to worry about me. I can manage very well on my own," the stranger said as they reached the back fence of Melissa's yard.

"Missy!" Mr. Ballard called from the kitchen window. "Time for dinner!"

"Just a minute," Melissa replied. But when she turned back, the spacegirl was already bounding across the field.

Melissa watched her disappear with a pang of regret. She realized she hadn't even asked her name.

16

"Some people I simply don't understand," said Mr. Ballard. "The man is an internationally respected scientist, and he was screaming at me like a four-year-old."

Even as a four-year-old, Melissa couldn't remember screaming at her father. She tried to imagine it: a little man in a white lab coat stamping his foot and yelling like Rumpelstiltskin.

"He must have been very upset," said Mrs. Ballard.

"So was I. He didn't even have the good manners to shut the door."

The Ballards were all seated around the polished walnut table in the dining room, eating Mr. Ballard's take-out choice-of-the-week, Thai food. As they did each night, they were also reporting what had hap-

pened to them that day. Once again, Mr. Ballard's day
had not been a good one. The chemistry department
he'd come west to head was swamped with problems
that were keeping him from the laboratory research
that was his real love. Molecules never yelled at him
or threw tantrums.

"I don't need this kind of aggravation," he said, and
sighed.

"No one does," agreed Mrs. Ballard, probably thinking of her own boss, the cranky chairman of the board
who never seemed happy with the speeches that she
wrote. Tonight she would have to work late again at
home to revise a speech he was to deliver tomorrow
at an insurance conference.

"What about your day?" she asked Melissa. "Tell us
something cheery."

Would they be happy to hear about her twilight
encounter? Or would it just upset them? "My day was
okay," she replied, her customary answer.

"Okay how?" Mrs. Ballard prodded.

"I got a hundred and three on my math test," she
offered.

"Schools have certainly changed since I was a boy,"
said Mr. Ballard, grinning from behind his shaggy, salt-
and-pepper beard. "It was enough to get a hundred
then."

"Everything is bigger and better in California." Mrs.
Ballard smiled.

"I keep forgetting," he said.

Mrs. Ballard turned to Melissa. "It hasn't taken you long to catch on. We should all be doing as well." She looked at her husband as if she were going to say something more; instead, she passed the beef and broccoli.

"Of course, she's doing well," Mr. Ballard said. "Why shouldn't she? A bright girl in a terrific school, with a wonderful violin teacher. And nobody yelling at her every day."

Melissa buried her broccoli under little mounds of rice.

"You know what would be nice," Mrs. Ballard suggested, "to invite some of your new friends over so we could meet them. Maybe this weekend . . ."

Outside, a blur of white flashed by the window.

"Do you think there's life on other planets?" Melissa asked abruptly.

"Now that's an interesting question," said Mr. Ballard, who always enjoyed a good scientific debate.

Mrs. Ballard looked puzzled. "Is this something you're studying at school?"

"I have to do a science report," Melissa lied.

"Well, extraterrestrial life is a fascinating subject," Mr. Ballard said. "In our galaxy alone, there are about one hundred billion stars. . . ."

Behind him the girl in the space suit raised her head and peered in the window, pressing her stub nose to the glass. Had she changed her mind about New York?

"At least ten percent of those stars have planets, and maybe one percent of those have Earth-like conditions that would support life as we know it," Mr. Ballard went on. "So it would be against the law of averages if life hadn't formed on some fraction of those planets."

"You mean like E.T.?" said Mrs. Ballard, who often became impatient with her husband's lectures. "You think there are millions of fuzzy little creatures living in outer space?"

"They could be fuzzy, they could be bald. There's no way of telling," Mr. Ballard answered.

"How about smarter?" Melissa asked, trying to distract her parents from the moonlike face watching them through the window.

"No way to predict that either. They could be a million years ahead of us or a million years behind."

The spacegirl rolled her varicolored eyes. Apparently she didn't think that Mr. Ballard was very advanced either.

"If they're smarter than we are, wouldn't they try to visit us?" Melissa continued.

"So far there's no scientifically credible evidence that they have. Of course, maybe it's a sign of their intelligence that they haven't." Mr. Ballard chuckled.

Or maybe they just don't want to talk to scientists, Melissa thought, but didn't say.

Outside, the spacegirl broke into a grin, then sprang into the air and disappeared as if she'd leaped over the house.

Melissa pushed her chair away from the table. "Can I be excused?" she asked.

"I have a good dessert tonight—ice cream and chocolate sauce," Mr. Ballard bribed.

"I'm full," Melissa answered, getting up.

"You feeling all right?" Mrs. Ballard asked, concerned.

"I'm fine. I have that report to do," she lied again, "and I haven't practiced yet." Homework and the violin excused almost anything for her parents.

She hurried upstairs to her bedroom and shut the door. Then she stepped outside to the deck to survey the backyard. There was no sign of the stranger. She checked the sloping rooftop beside her balcony. No visitor there either. She glanced up at the sky. In New York there were so many lights that it was hard to see the stars. Here the nights were black and clear and sparkled with a billion stars.

"Two stars to the right of the Little Dipper; that's our sun." A reedy voice spoke to her in the dark.

Startled, Melissa turned to see the spacegirl squatting on a branch of the eucalyptus tree that grew a few yards from the house.

"I thought you were going to New York," Melissa said.

"I am. When I'm ready. But I don't like being rushed."

"Nobody's rushing you. I just asked a simple question."

"Questions are never simple. If they were, no one would have to ask them." The girl stood up on her tree branch. "Earth is very strange," she said. "On Zironia we always welcome travelers. We want to learn about their planets. Aren't you curious about Zironia?"

"Of course I am," Melissa said. There were hundreds of things she wanted to know.

"Really?" In one deft motion the girl grabbed the limb above her and swung to the deck as easily as a chimpanzee. "Like what?"

"Can you fly?"

The girl laughed; a sharp, pealing sound that echoed like a bell through the clear night air. "If I could, do you think I'd still be here? I'd be strolling down Fifth Avenue right this minute. Now it's my turn to ask. How come your parents are so unhappy?"

Melissa gasped. "How do you know that?"

"I watched through the window. You lie much better than they do."

"My parents"—Melissa took a deep breath—"are still getting used to this place."

"So that's why you didn't tell them about me."

"I didn't tell them because they wouldn't understand. You heard my father. He doesn't think you're scientifically credible."

"And what do you think?"

They stood a few feet apart staring at each other. The girl's eyes had darkened and were all pupils now, like a cat's, and she smelled of eucalyptus and of a more exotic perfume that Melissa couldn't quite place.

"I think you're scared of me," the spacegirl answered her own question.

"No," Melissa denied, forgetting that the girl could read her thoughts.

"You don't need to be frightened. Zironians are very peaceful people. We haven't had a war on our planet for centuries."

"That's good to hear," said Melissa, not completely reassured. War was not what she was worrying about.

The girl looked past Melissa to her bedroom. "Well, aren't you going to invite me in?"

"What's wrong with talking out here?"

"It looks warmer inside."

Melissa hesitated, studying the girl's milky face and punklike haircut and earrings.

"My parents wouldn't approve."

"Parents never approve. That's their job."

"Yours don't either?"

The girl shrugged the oversized shoulders of her spacesuit. "Why do you think they sent me to Earth?"

"Why?"

"Because I have some *very important lessons* to learn."

"What kind of lessons?"

The girl shook her head. "No, you've had your question. It's my turn again. When your parents don't approve, what do you do?"

"Most of the time I do what they tell me," Melissa confessed.

"I can see that."

"Well, you don't have to be mean about it," Melissa said defensively.

"You're too touchy. On Zironia we'd say, 'Take a walk on Urzu.' That's our moon, where the gravity is lighter."

"On Earth we say, 'Lighten up.' " Melissa smiled.

"Well, lighten up, missy." She laughed her bell-like laugh.

"I don't even know your name," Melissa said.

"It's Solay."

"Mine's Melissa." She extended her hand. "When people meet here, they shake hands." She gestured to show how.

"I know," Solay nodded. She removed a white glove and took Melissa's hand. The spacegirl's fingers were long and thin and very cold.

"When people meet on Zironia, they touch heads." She brushed her forehead lightly against Melissa's. Again Melissa caught the exotic scent.

"Can we go inside?" Solay asked.

"Just for a little while," Melissa said, opening the sliding door. "Until you get warm."

Solay followed her inside and immediately plopped on the white eyelet bedspread on Melissa's bed.

"You can't do that!" Melissa objected. "You'll get the bedspread dirty."

Solay paid no attention. She stretched out with her dirty boots and space suit and shut her eyes. "It's been such a long day." She sighed.

"Don't you dare fall asleep on me," Melissa warned. Too late. Solay's body had already relaxed into the deep, rhythmic breathing of sleep.

Melissa slumped into her reading chair and studied the strange person on her bed.

This is a big mistake, she thought. Tomorrow she's going to have to go.

A t five minutes to seven the next morning, Melissa
bolted up in bed. Solay lay like a stone beside her.
Melissa shook her heavily padded shoulders. "C'mon,
get up," she urged.

Solay burrowed deeper under the covers.

Melissa shook her again, harder. In a few minutes
her mother would come in to make sure she was
awake.

Solay rolled over on her back, and her eyes blinked
open. "Do you always treat guests this roughly?"

"I invited you in to talk, not to sleep over," Melissa
said.

Solay stretched and scratched her stubby hair.
"Well, we can talk now."

"There's no time now. I have to go to school."

Solay sat up. "I can come with you," she said brightly.

"No way!"

"Why not?"

"A million reasons."

"Name one."

"You can't go to school in a space suit."

"I'll change," Solay said easily. "I'll wear something of yours."

Melissa heard her mother's footsteps approaching. "Quick, under the covers." She threw the quilt over Solay's head and sat on her to make sure she wouldn't escape.

Mrs. Ballard entered in her bathrobe, carrying a coffee cup. From the dark pockets under her gray eyes, Melissa guessed she'd been up late last night rewriting Mr. Stohlmyer's speech. "Good, you're awake. You'll need to hurry—your father has an early meeting."

Solay squirmed.

Melissa bounced on the wiggling covers. "Okay, I'll be right down."

"I wish I had your energy this morning," Mrs. Ballard said wearily.

Underneath the quilt, Solay jabbed her. Melissa jumped.

"Are you okay?" Mrs. Ballard gave her a suspicious look.

"Fine." Melissa bounded from the bed and steered her mother toward the door.

Mrs. Ballard lingered a moment. "I brought your new dress back from the cleaners."

"I have something else picked out for today," Melissa answered. The Fashion Critics had dismissed the dress her mother had bought her as a *Little House on the Prairie* hand-me-down."

"Whatever you want," Mrs. Ballard said, clearly disappointed.

Melissa shut the door behind her.

Like a pale moon emerging from behind the clouds, Solay's head rose from beneath the sheets. "You really are a good liar," she said.

"I *was* thinking of wearing something else," Melissa protested.

"I'm glad I can read your thoughts."

"Then you know you're nothing but trouble."

"I'm not trouble," Solay said, unruffled. "I'm excitement."

"I don't need excitement either." Melissa opened her closet. At the private school she'd attended in New York, everyone wore uniforms, but at Emerson Elementary the students followed a more complicated dress code. The unwritten rules were strictly enforced. The first rule was always wear name brands.

Melissa's closet was filled with the right labels, but she always had trouble with the second rule— matching them correctly.

Today there was no time to choose. She picked out a maroon skirt and a lavender shirt, a safe combination because she'd worn them a week before without provoking any comment.

Solay sat cross-legged on the bed, watching her. She focused her eyes on a yellow jersey Melissa had thrown on a chair. The jersey rose into the air and floated over to her.

Melissa gaped. "What are you doing?"

Solay held up the jersey in front of her. "This goes better with that skirt."

"How did you do that?"

"What?" Solay said innocently.

"You know perfectly what. How did you make that jersey fly through the air?"

"Oh, that's simple. Just mind over matter. Thought waves converted into energy. Clothes are easy to move. . . ." She demonstrated by drawing an orange blouse over from the dresser.

So she had unearthly powers after all.

"Stop showing off!" Melissa cried.

"That's not showing off," Solay said. "Showing off would be moving that chair." She stared at it and narrowed her eyes.

Melissa leaped in front of the chair. "Don't! Please don't," she begged.

"You're very jumpy this morning." Solay hopped off the bed and approached the closet. She found a hot pink skirt on the floor and tried it with the orange top.

"Now that really goes together," she exclaimed.

And my mother thinks my taste is bad, Melissa marveled.

"What's taste?" Solay asked.

"Taste," Melissa said impatiently, "is like manners. If you have good taste, you always pick the proper thing to wear."

"Oh, *prop*-er." Solay gave the word an exaggerated pronunciation.

"I suppose on Zironia you wear whatever you want," Melissa snapped.

"Most of the time we don't wear any clothes at all."

"No wonder you can't match," Melissa said.

"Why is matching so important?" Solay asked.

"Because if you wear the wrong clothes, you stick out."

Solay tilted her head sassily. "I like sticking out."

"Well, I *don't*," Melissa said.

Solay hopped back onto the bed. "Being *prop*-er is boring," she said.

"Missy, hurry up! I can't be late," Mr. Ballard called from the kitchen.

"You have any earrings?" Solay asked, fixing her eyes on the jewelry box on Melissa's dresser. The lid popped open. Melissa quickly shut it. "Look," she said, trying hard to be stern. "You can't stay here any longer. I'm going to school. My parents are going to work."

"Go," Solay urged. "I can manage on my own."

Melissa was unsure how much to trust her.

"Don't worry, I won't get you into trouble," Solay added.

"What will you do?" Melissa asked.

The corners of Solay's mouth turned up. "Oh, I'm going to enjoy being different." She began to unzip her space suit.

"You'd better stay in my room until we leave," Melissa warned.

"Or what?" Solay asked.

"Or . . ." Unable to come up with a good answer, Melissa slammed the door. Whether by magic or not, the door swung open again, revealing a pale Solay tumbling naked on the bed, flipping through the air as weightlessly as a ghost.

Melissa closed the door firmly and went downstairs.

As usual, her parents were trying to do several things at once. Mrs. Ballard, now ready except for makeup, was packing Melissa's lunch and dictating a dinner recipe for Elena, their Guatemalan housekeeper. Mr. Ballard was printing the recipe in capital letters as he drank his morning coffee and waited for the bread to toast. He handed Melissa half a grapefruit.

Mrs. Ballard looked up from the chicken sandwich she was making. "You know what would go well with that—your new argyle socks."

Melissa had carelessly put on white ones. For once

31

her mother was right. "I'll get them," she said.

"Food before socks," Mr. Ballard commanded. "Sit down and eat your breakfast. You can't do a good day's work on an empty stomach."

"I'll bring them down," Mrs. Ballard volunteered.

"No!" Melissa cried.

Her mother looked at her in surprise.

"I agree," Mr. Ballard said, interpreting Melissa's alarm in his own way. "You can't leave Elena without instructions for dinner. That's a recipe for heartburn." Even with instructions in easy-to-read English, Elena's cooking was generally terrible.

"I'll write out the recipe later," said Mrs. Ballard, snapping Melissa's lunchbox closed.

As she started for the stairs, the phone rang. She stopped and whispered frantically to Mr. Ballard, "Say I've already left." But he didn't seem to hear.

"Just a minute," he said to the caller and held out the phone. "It's your office."

Scowling, Mrs. Ballard took the receiver. "Yes, Mr. Stohlmyer . . . certainly. Let me get a pencil to write that down. . . ." She glared again at her husband, who shrugged helplessly.

Melissa finished her grapefruit and rose from the table.

"Where are you going?" Mr. Ballard said sharply.

"To get my socks."

"No time." He caught her by her shoulders and

turned her toward the kitchen door. "We're already five minutes late. You can eat your toast in the car."

"You start the car, Dad. I'll get the socks and meet you outside."

He shook his head. "There's nothing wrong with white socks. White goes with everything. It includes all the colors of the spectrum."

There was no use arguing. Now Melissa wished she had Solay's powers and could float the socks downstairs with a wave of her hand.

Mr. Ballard waved good-bye to his wife, who ignored him but blew a kiss to Melissa. "Yes, I've got that . . ." she said into the phone. Then she whispered, "Don't forget your violin."

Melissa grabbed her backpack and violin case and left the house.

As Mr. Ballard backed the station wagon out of the garage, she glanced up at the balcony of her bedroom. Solay was standing there, watching them. She was wearing Melissa's pink skirt, yellow jersey, and the argyle knee socks Mrs. Ballard had suggested. As garish as Solay looked, Melissa was relieved that she'd at least had the decency to get dressed before stepping outside.

5

Mrs. Rademacher was a big fan of theme-teach-ing—linking all school subjects to the same topic. For Thanksgiving the class was studying the Pilgrims (history); learning about turkeys (science); drawing a mural of the first Thanksgiving (art); and now English. This morning's assignment was an in-class composition on "What I Have to Be Thankful For."

The groan from the students suggested that few would put Mrs. Rademacher on their lists. Melissa wasn't feeling particularly thankful either this morn-ing, but she bent her head to her notebook, thinking what she could write that would please her teacher. She was still writing when Mrs. Rademacher told them to bring their essays to a close.

"Now who would like to read his or her composition?" the teacher asked.

No one volunteered.

"I can't believe that *none* of you has reasons to be thankful," she gently chided them. She searched the room for someone she knew had reasons to be happy. Her eyes came to rest on the prettiest girl in the class.

Rochelle rose reluctantly and read her essay. She was grateful for her pretty house, her many clothes, and her small feet.

Eager to outdo her, others now waved their hands. Caitlin was thankful that she lived in such a beautiful community as Crestwood Estates and went to such a good school as Emerson and had such a fine teacher as Mrs. Rademacher and that she wasn't living in Pilgrim times when the clothes were all so drab.

Dougie was happy that his father had moved out of the house and couldn't yell at his mother anymore.

David was happy that he lived in America, a country where anyone could be successful if he worked hard enough.

Melissa kept her head lowered, her eyes focused on her desk, hoping Mrs. Rademacher would overlook her. It didn't work. "What about you, Melissa? Could you share your thoughts with us?"

Quickly and with a dry mouth, Melissa read her composition. "Whenever I feel unhappy, I think of the old man who used to live on our street in New York.

In the summer he slept in a doorway. In the winter he slept on a steam grate to keep warm. He wore the same clothes every day and always looked dirty. Sometimes my father would give him money when we passed. He always said, 'God bless you.' One day he disappeared. I often wonder what happened to him, and if he found a home somewhere. Whenever I think of him I realize how fortunate I am. There are many people in the world who don't have enough to eat or a bed to sleep in or clothes to keep them warm. I've never had to worry about any of those things. I'm very thankful my life has been so easy."

When Melissa looked up, Mrs. Rademacher's eyes were damp. She dabbed at one of them with a corner of her shawl. "That was very touching, Melissa. It shows a very generous spirit. Your essay reminds us to be compassionate to those less fortunate than we are. You have set a Thanksgiving example for us all. All right, class, now please pass your compositions forward."

Melissa passed her paper down the row of desks. When it reached Caitlin, she deliberately let it fall to the floor, then stepped on it and rubbed it with her shoe. "Oh, sorry!" she said. Turning back to Melissa, she whispered, "I hope Miss Generous can forgive me."

Melissa busied herself with her notebook and tried to pretend she didn't care. She didn't know why they were so mean to her. She wasn't trying to show them up. She had just wanted to do what Mrs. Rademacher asked.

At noon when she went to her locker, she knew that they had gotten their revenge. There were too many kids hanging around the hall unable to hide their grins. Nervously she picked up her lunchbox. It felt empty! They had stolen her food. And now they were waiting to gloat.

She couldn't do anything about her lunch, but she could at least ruin their celebration. She put the lunchbox back in her locker without opening it. She felt the rustle of disappointment in the corridor.

"Going on a diet?" a girl behind her snickered.

"Giving your lunch to the homeless?"

Melissa turned and started for the door. Sally Gillkey hurried after her.

"You want to share my sandwich?" she offered. Reaching into a paper bag, she brought forth half a messy bologna sandwich oozing mayonnaise.

Melissa looked at it, feeling sick. "Thanks," she said, "but I'm allergic to bologna."

She fled through the door and into the school yard. Sally and the others trailed behind her. With nowhere to escape in the playground, she headed for the gate. Without breaking stride or looking back, she marched out of the school yard and down the street.

Halfway down the block, she glanced back over

her shoulder. Sally Gillkey was still standing by the chain-link fence, but the others had gone on to better games. Melissa crossed the street and cut through an empty lot that hadn't yet been bulldozed for construction.

"You don't have to run. I haven't left yet." A familiar voice floated down to Melissa like a cool breeze tingling the back of her neck.

Looking up, she spotted her new, high-top, red tennis shoes dangling from the branch of a pepper tree. Solay waggled the Reeboks at her in greeting.

"It's polite to ask before borrowing things," Melissa said.

"You didn't want me to go naked, did you?" Solay parted the pepper branches to reveal the rest of her outfit. She was now wearing pink tights, blue Bermuda shorts, and a green-striped blouse—a combination that would have struck the Fashion Critics dumb. Melissa didn't know what to say herself.

"Say, 'It's colorful.' " Solay sprang from the tree and landed on the ground as lightly as a cat.

"It's certainly that," Melissa agreed.

Solay folded her arms and leaned against the tree. "I thought you'd be happier to see me."

"I'm having a bad day," Melissa grumbled.

"Well, are you going to ruin the rest of it sulking?"

"They stole my lunch!"

"Who did?"

"Celia, Rochelle, Caitlin, David . . . it could've been any of them . . . or all of them."

"So what are you going to do about it?"

"What can I do?" Melissa shrugged.

"No wonder they took it!" Solay spread her hands and did a few easy cartwheels on the grass. She whirled to a stop in front of Melissa. "Do you always let people pick on you?"

"Not *always*."

"Just most of the time, right?"

"How can I stop them? They all hate me."

"A *proper* girl like you? You're so sweet, so generous. Why would they hate you?" Solay did another cartwheel.

"They're jealous."

Solay rested her pale hands on her bright Bermuda shorts and studied Melissa. "Of what? Why would they be jealous of *you*?"

"Because I'm so smart," Melissa said, flustered.

"Then how come you can't get them to stop picking on you?" Solay smiled and did a backflip, landing perfectly on the balls of her feet.

Melissa wanted to shove her in the chest and knock her over.

Solay backed up a step. "Oh, Miss Proper can get angry after all."

"If it was your problem, you'd be angry too."

"If it was my problem, I'd solve it," Solay said confidently.

"How?"

About to do another cartwheel, Solay stopped. "You asking me to help?"

"I guess I am," Melissa realized. "Would you?"

"I might. I have nothing better to do right now. But if I help you out, you have to help me in return."

"How?" Melissa said uneasily.

"Help me get to New York."

"That's too hard," she complained. "I don't know how to do that."

"It's easy. Come with me."

"It may be different in Zironia," Melissa reasoned, "but in America ten-year-olds don't run away from home. Especially when they have no money. It's not practical."

Solay shrugged. "Too bad. I know so many good ways to stop bullies."

"That's because you are one yourself," Melissa said, discouraged.

Solay laughed. "I offer to make a fair exchange, and you call me a bully. That's not very nice . . . or generous."

"Your offer wasn't fair," Melissa protested. "How can I get you to New York?"

"How do you know until you try?" Solay asked.

The school bell rang down the street, announcing

the end of lunch. Melissa sighed. Although she didn't want to return, she was afraid not to.

She started back toward the school yard. Solay sauntered beside her.

"Are you sure you can help me?" Melissa asked.

"Does Zironia have two moons?" Solay asked.

"How do I know?" Melissa said in exasperation. "I never even heard of Zironia until last night."

"Well, it does," Solay assured her. "Urzu and Zuru."

"What if I can't get you to New York?"

"You're stuck with me until you do."

Passing a tree inside a fenced yard, Solay waved her hand and a plump orange floated down. She started peeling the skin. "Of course, I could always find somebody else to help me."

Across the street Melissa's classmates were already heading inside the building. Several of them were standing on the steps, surveying the neighborhood. Were they waiting to see if she was coming back?

She really could use some extraterrestrial help.

"Okay," Melissa agreed. "I'll give New York some thought."

Solay smiled and tossed her the orange. "Good," she said. "Now you'd better eat. You'll need your strength to fight back."

41

6

"No, no, no, Melissa." Mr. Hofheinz tapped his slender forefinger on the armrest of his black wooden rocker. "It is not enough to play the right notes. You must feel the phrasing. Again, please."

Melissa repositioned the violin beneath her chin, took a deep breath, and began the piece again. She had been struggling with the Courante section of Bach's Partita No. 2 in D Minor for a month now, and despite all her practice, still wasn't able to please Mr. Hofheinz.

Leaning back in his chair, he crossed his slender legs. A retired symphony violinist, he always wore a tie and suit jacket to impress upon his students the seriousness of their lessons.

Melissa focused her eyes on the music on the stand in front of her. "Music gives you faith in the essential order of the universe," Mr. Ballard liked to say. Having studied the violin since she was five, Melissa often tried to imagine what he meant. But the hundreds of hours she spent practicing scales and études only made her think of endless rows of fence posts.

"All right, my dear, with feeling!" Mr. Hofheinz pressed his pale hands together as if praying for her.

This time she tried to put all her energy into it. Turning the page of the music, she glanced out the window. Solay was sitting on top of the teacher's wooden fence, holding her nose.

Melissa lost her place.

Mr. Hofheinz tapped the armrest again. "You are distracted today, no?"

"No . . . yes . . . a little," Melissa conceded.

"Your mind is elsewhere?" Mr. Hofheinz asked kindly. Although her playing made him frown, he never lost his patience with her.

Outside Solay mimed playing a violin, shook her head, and tossed the imaginary fiddle over the fence.

"Or maybe it is the Bach you do not like?"

"It is not my favorite," she admitted.

"Ah, such a delightful piece. It is so light, so graceful, like skipping through the park on a sunny day. You must play it that way."

Melissa tried to remember the last time she had

43

skipped anywhere. It must have been months ago, before her parents even thought of leaving New York. But she didn't see how that could help her play Bach.

"The Courante is a dance, not a technical exercise." Mr. Hofheinz hummed a few bars and waved his hand to illustrate.

Melissa craned her neck to watch Solay.

"Something outside?" Mr. Hofheinz turned to the window.

"Just a cat," Melissa replied as Solay disappeared from view.

"Well, now we concentrate on music, all right? Begin again, please." He tapped his chair.

Wearily, Melissa raised her bow.

"You're very quiet this evening," Mrs. Ballard said as she drove Melissa home.

"So are you."

"Sorry, I guess I'm tired." Mrs. Ballard brushed her long hair back from her face, a gesture that Melissa had noticed more and more lately. She'd also noticed several gray streaks in her mother's auburn hair. "Thinking about a new speech for Mr. Stohlmyer?" she asked.

"Actually, I was thinking about Paris," Mrs. Ballard said with a half-smile.

Melissa's mother had majored in French in college and after graduation had worked for a while in Paris.

"What about Paris?" Melissa asked. She liked hearing stories of her mother's adventures in France. Her mother seemed different then.

"Oh, I was just thinking how far away it is."

"You ever sorry you came back?"

"No, I couldn't have stayed in France," Mrs. Ballard answered without regret. "Anyway I fell in love with your father. So I moved to New York to marry him. In the beginning living there was a challenge, but it turned out fine. Although change can be hard sometimes, it's exciting, too."

Her mother could always find something to be positive about. Melissa wished she was more like her in that way.

"So what happened at school today?" Mrs. Ballard asked.

Melissa hesitated. Her mother liked difficult challenges. Maybe she could help. "A girl's lunch got stolen," Melissa said cautiously.

"Really. Whose?"

"Her name's . . . Sally. Sally Gillkey."

"Why did they steal her lunch?"

"She doesn't know why. Or who did it. She asked me what to do. I didn't know what to tell her."

Mrs. Ballard stopped at a traffic light and considered the problem. She looked over at Melissa. "Has this happened a lot?"

"A couple of times." Melissa avoided her mother's glance.

"Has she gone to the teacher?"

"No, she doesn't want to do that," Melissa said quickly. "That'll just make things worse."

"Sally could ask Mrs. Rademacher not to say anything about it in class."

"No, if Mrs. Rademacher did anything, they'd know and get even."

Mrs. Ballard ran her hand through her hair again. "It would be easier to suggest something if I knew why they were picking on Sally."

"Because they're mean and they're bullies," Melissa said with conviction.

"And Sally doesn't fight back . . ."

Melissa nodded.

"Well, two are stronger than one. Maybe together you can stop them. What if you kept Sally's lunch in your locker?"

"Maybe," Melissa mumbled.

"Or you could hide it your backpack." Mrs. Ballard was suddenly full of suggestions. "She's sure lucky about one thing," Mrs. Ballard concluded. "That she has you for a friend. You should invite her over next week so I can meet her."

"I'll ask her," Melissa lied, sorry that she'd mentioned it. Why did she think her mother could help anyway? She couldn't even talk back to Mr. Stohlmyer.

Solay didn't reappear until after dinner, when Melissa found her sitting cross-legged on her bed, wearing a black sweater and Melissa's new jeans. She seemed to be fast making up for all those years of running around naked on Zironia.

"You figured out how to get me out of here?" Solay asked.

"I've had a few other things to do."

"Why don't you sell your violin? I bet that would earn enough money to buy us both plane tickets."

"I can't sell my violin."

"Why not? You can't play it."

Melissa grabbed her yellow jersey from the chair and threw it at her. Solay deftly moved her head to the side and the shirt sailed past.

"Temper! Temper!" she laughed.

"I don't like you making fun of me," Melissa said angrily. "It's my room, my house, my planet. Why don't you go home?"

Solay shrugged. "I can't."

"What do you mean, you can't?"

"I can't return until my parents come back for me."

"When will that be?"

"When I've learned the lessons I'm supposed to," she said simply.

"What lessons?"

"How will I know until I've learned them?" Solay replied, tucking her head and somersaulting on the bed.

Melissa sank into her armchair in frustration. "You could be here for years!" she said.

"Not if I help you out," Solay reminded her. "I tickle

your toes, you tickle mine. That's the Zironian way."
She dropped her feet to the floor. "*You* may not have
done anything useful this afternoon, but *I*'ve figured
out how to solve your lunch problem."

"Really?" Melissa said skeptically.

"Sure. What's the gnarliest thing you can think of?"

"The gnarliest?" Two days on Earth and already she
was speaking slang, Melissa noted.

"Yeah, the grossest thing you can think of . . ."

"Dougie Drollinger picking his nose in class and
playing with his boogers."

"That's gross, all right," Solay chirped. "But it won't
work. Think of something else."

"Snails."

"Good. That'll do it."

"Snails?"

"Right. Where do we find them?"

"Outside. They're all over the garden."

"Great. Let's collect some."

"But how's that going to help?" Melissa asked,
confused.

"It's an old Zironian trick. If you get some snails,
I'll show you." Solay pulled a sweater from Melissa's
dresser and threw it to her. "Now let's go."

Melissa was too curious not to follow. She opened
the bedroom door and peered downstairs. Her parents
were both in the kitchen doing the dinner dishes.

"I'm taking one of my TV hours," she called down

48

to them, and turned on the television set in her parents' bedroom. Then she grabbed a flashlight and a paper bag and quietly stole down the steps with Solay.

Outside, the front lawn was still wet from the Ballards' automatic sprinklers and the damp grass was full of snail tracks. The beam of Melissa's flashlight exposed the snails' slimy little heads and squishy bodies emerging from their shells.

"What are you waiting for?" Solay asked. "Pick some up."

"You pick them up," Melissa replied. "This was your idea."

"But it's your lunch problem."

"I don't like touching them. They're slimy."

"*Magi!*" Solay exclaimed. "Take them by the shell." She demonstrated how.

Gingerly, with her fingertips, Melissa picked up a snail shell and dropped it in the bag.

"Now was that so bad?" Solay said.

"What are we going to do with them?" Melissa asked.

Solay smiled mysteriously. "You'll see," she said.

In the morning, Melissa woke early, jangly with nerves and anticipation. The night before, she and Solay had stayed awake a long time carefully working out all the steps of Solay's plan. It was a wonderful scheme.

Solay was already up and dressed, wearing Melissa's new jeans and an orange shirt over a black T-shirt, a combination Melissa wished she had thought to wear herself. "Hey, I was going to wear those jeans today," she protested.

Solay admired herself in the mirror on the back of the closet door. "Too bad I picked them first."

She handed Melissa an old pair of Levi's and a brown shirt. "Here, this looks drab enough. You don't want to call attention to yourself by wearing anything unusual."

"I'll pick out my own clothes, thank you," Melissa said, looking for another shirt.

"How about something snail-colored?" Solay laughed.

"Your plan had better work!" Melissa muttered.

"It will, if you don't mess it up."

Why was it that Solay always seemed to have the last word? Melissa wondered.

"Because you let me," Solay replied with a grin.

The night before, they'd hidden the snails behind a bush alongside the garage. It was easy for Melissa to pick up the bag and stuff it inside her backpack while her father backed the Volvo out of the garage.

Solay watched approvingly from the deck outside Melissa's bedroom. "See you at school," she called as Melissa climbed into the car.

That worried Melissa as much as the snails. Just how and when was Solay going to show up?

Inside the car, Melissa kept glancing at the backpack by her feet to see if any snails were creeping out. Or was the Brahms that her father was playing forcing them deeper into their shells? Could snails hear anyway? she wondered. At another time she would ask her father.

"Ah, Brahms!" he exclaimed as he turned down

School Lane. "Music to wash away the dust of daily life."

"You can just let me off at the corner," Melissa said.

"Why?" he asked, slowing the car. Her father needed an explanation for everything.

"Because . . . I'm meeting somebody. Please, right here," she said impatiently.

"Whatever you say." He braked the car. "When I was your age I had secrets, too."

Melissa grabbed her backpack and hastily opened the door.

He watched her a moment through the window. Then a passage of music caught his attention, and he raised his finger to follow the orchestra and drove away.

As soon as he was gone, Melissa ducked behind some shrubbery. First she emptied her lunch into a fresh paper bag. Then she dumped the snails into the lunchbox and hid the paper sack in a branch of the pepper tree where she had met Solay the day before. She waited until two minutes before the bell and then hurried to school. After shoving her backpack and lunchbox into her locker, she strolled into class, trying to look as calm as possible.

There was nothing to do now but wait.

Halfway through math Dougie wiggled his hand for permission to go to the bathroom.

Mrs. Rademacher frowned over her glasses. "You've

been here barely forty-five minutes, Douglas."

"Please, Mrs. Rademacher," he begged, squirming.

"All right, but be quick about it," the teacher relented.

"Yeah, come back for lunch," a boy muttered under his breath.

The class tittered as Dougie left the room, slamming the door loudly.

Melissa rubbed her hands nervously over her knees. Was he the thief?

Five minutes later Dougie sauntered back, looking as bored as when he'd left. Clearly he was not the thief.

The morning dragged on as slowly as the minute hand on the clock. Solay was nowhere in sight.

"Melissa?"

"Yes!" Mrs. Rademacher's voice startled her.

"I was asking about the Pilgrims," Mrs. Rademacher explained. They had shifted from math to social studies.

"The Pilgrims . . ." Melissa had no idea what her question had been.

"Are you with us this morning, Melissa?" Mrs. Rademacher asked gently.

"She's thinking about the homeless, ma'am," Celia volunteered.

Mrs. Rademacher silenced the burst of laughter with a stern look. "We are discussing the relations between the colonists and the Indians," she reminded everyone.

David almost leaped out of his seat to answer.

Mrs. Rademacher called on him, and he repeated, almost word-for-word, the explanation in their textbook. Afterward he glanced at Melissa with a superior smile.

She hoped he'd try to steal her lunch today. Then he'd find out who was really smart.

At recess, Melissa went outside with the rest of the class, but she stayed close to the door by the lockers in case David or anyone else made his move. Perhaps her presence scared them off, though, because at the end of recess, her lunchbox was in the exact spot she'd placed it that morning.

By lunchtime Melissa began to fear that Solay's trap was going to fail. After all their planning, maybe no one would try to steal her lunch today.

When the noon bell rang, she lingered in her seat to give her classmates one last opportunity.

A shrill scream sounded in the hall. The thief alarm.

Melissa rushed out the door to catch her tormentor.

Her lunchbox was upside down in her locker and snails were scattered all over the floor. Caitlin was fiercely stomping them to the cheers of the other fifth graders.

"Oh, gross!" Caitlin cried in disgust, as she brought her foot down again on another shell.

At the end of the hall, Solay perched triumphantly on top of the arts-and-crafts display case. She waved at Melissa. Everyone else was too busy enjoying Caitlin's snail-stomping to notice.

Caitlin ground another snail into the floor with her heel and glared at Melissa as if she'd like to do the same to her.

"What's going on here?" demanded Mrs. Rademacher, who had followed Melissa into the hall.

All the children looked at Caitlin, waiting to see how she would talk her way out of this. On top of the arts-and-crafts case, Solay beamed.

"It's her fault!" Caitlin pointed to Melissa. "She's putting snails in our lunches."

Melissa paled. This wasn't the way the plan was supposed to work.

"Is that true, Melissa?" Mrs. Rademacher removed her glasses to look at her.

Though she wanted to scream "*No,*" Melissa's mouth refused to open. She looked to the top of the arts-and-crafts cabinet for help from Solay, but Solay was no longer there.

"Look in her lunchbox!" Caitlin cried.

Mrs. Rademacher looked from Caitlin to Melissa, trying to judge the truth. "Let me see your lunchbox, Melissa," she said quietly.

Melissa's hand trembled as she picked up the lunchbox and gave it to the teacher. Mrs. Rademacher cautiously lifted the lid and then quickly shut it, but not fast enough to keep everyone from seeing the few snails left inside.

"She's been putting them in our lunches, too," Celia jumped in, delighted to be able to help Caitlin out.

"Look at your sandwiches," Caitlin warned. "Maybe she stuck snails in yours, too."

The others immediately started tearing open their lunches to see. Behind Mrs. Rademacher, Dougie picked up a snail from the floor and stuck it in his peanut butter and jelly sandwich.

"Oh, here's one!" Dougie pulled the gooey snail from his sandwich and held it a few inches from his mouth. "Do you think they taste good this way?"

"Yuck!"

"Sickening!"

"Try it!"

"Enough!" Mrs. Rademacher glared.

Among the children in the hall, only Sally Gillkey seemed to look at Melissa with sympathy. Yet Sally was as mute as she.

"All right, everyone, the fun is over," Mrs. Rademacher declared. "I want all of you, except Melissa, out on the playground for lunch. Melissa, get a broom and clean up here. And when you're finished, I want to see you back in my room."

"What about my sandwich?" Caitlin complained.

"You'll just have to share with someone else," the teacher snapped. "Now go outside."

"Yes, Mrs. Rademacher," Caitlin said obediently, then smirked at Melissa when the teacher had turned her back.

Melissa took a long time sweeping up the hallway. This was a worse disaster then she could ever have imagined. Never before had any teacher singled her out for punishment. And for it to be unfair besides!

Solay had been smart to disappear. If she were anywhere nearby, Melissa would have thrown all the snails at her instead of in the trash.

Mrs. Rademacher was eating her lunch when Melissa finally returned to the classroom. The teacher beckoned her over to the desk. "I don't understand this," she said, puzzled. "Would you like to explain it to me?"

Melissa hung her head. How could she explain Solay to Mrs. Rademacher?

"This is so unlike you," the teacher said. She put her hand on Melissa's shoulder. "The way to fight meanness is not to become mean yourself, dear."

"I'm sorry," Melissa apologized, knowing that's what she wanted to hear.

"All right, you just stay in today and share my sandwiches with me. And we'll forget all about this."

"Thank you, Mrs. Rademacher."

She looked out the window. There, at a safe distance, was Solay, sitting on the fence, shaking her head in disgust.

Solay was sitting on the branch of the pepper tree after school, waiting for Melissa when she came to pick up the lunch she had hidden that morning.

"Oh, I'm *so* sorry, Mrs. Rademacher. Please forgive me," Solay whined pitifully.

"I didn't say it like that," Melissa objected.

"I'm sorry," Solay mumbled, and bowed her head in exact imitation of Melissa's apology to her teacher. "Is that more like it?"

"What else could I have done?" Melissa asked.

"How about saying something when Caitlin blamed you?"

Melissa felt her stomach knotting again as it had when Caitlin had accused her. "I . . . she caught me by surprise."

"I don't know why you're so scared of her," Solay said, leaping lightly to the ground.

"I'm not scared of her."

"Right." Solay reached into Melissa's lunch bag and pulled out an apple. She took a bite.

"Hey, I wanted to eat that apple."

"You should've told me."

"I'm telling you now. Give it back!" Melissa tried to snatch it from her, but Solay danced away. "That's my apple." Melissa grabbed for it again.

Solay took another bite and twirled the apple by its stem, just out of Melissa's reach. Melissa lunged for it, knocking it to the ground. When she picked it up, it was covered with dirt.

"Look at what you've done now!" Melissa flung the grubby apple at Solay. The spacegirl ducked and the apple sailed into the street.

"You're not afraid to get mad at me." Solay grinned.

"Because you're just . . . bad news," Melissa sputtered. "I should never've listened to you. You don't care what anyone else thinks. You just do what you want. I bet that's why you're here. You got into so much trouble on Zironia that they sent you to Earth for punishment."

"We don't believe in punishment on Zironia," Solay said haughtily. "We believe in reeducation. I came here to become a better person."

"Well, you're off to a great start."

Solay flipped onto her hands and started walking on them. Upside down, she retorted, "My mistake's been spending so much time with you."

Melissa gave Solay a sharp push that toppled her backward on the grass. "Go home, then," Melissa said angrily. "I don't need your help."

Solay rose slowly and carefully brushed the grass and leaves from her orange shirt. "How stupid of me," she said. "Why would you need my help? You're perfect the way you are."

"I didn't say that," Melissa muttered.

"No, you just act it. Miss Perfect never makes any mistakes. She never gets into trouble . . . I think I'll go live with Caitlin for a while. She knows how to have fun. And her clothes are sharper than yours."

"Do whatever you want. See if I care."

"I could spend some time at David's, too, help him with his tests and make him smarter than you."

"You'll only get him into trouble. That's what you're really good at."

"We'll see." She started to take off her shirt.

"What are you doing?" Melissa exclaimed.

"Returning your clothes."

"Keep them. I don't want to wear anything you've touched, you . . . you . . ." She couldn't think of anything hurtful enough to say.

"Just call me impudent," Solay helped out. "Or improper. Now that's a *really* terrible thing to be." She smiled and skipped away.

The pale alien was surrounded by the planetary police. The green-uniformed troops began to close in. . . . Melissa pushed the peas forward with her knife.

"Don't play with your food, Melissa."

"What?" Melissa looked up from her plate.

"If you don't like the peas and onions, don't eat them," Mrs. Ballard criticized. "But it's not polite to play with your food."

"What's so important about being polite?" Melissa asked.

Mr. Ballard put down his fork in surprise. "That's a strange question."

"Why? Why do you have to be polite all the time?" Melissa insisted.

"Being polite is a sign of respect for other people," Mrs. Ballard explained.

"How would you feel if someone came to dinner, ate with her hands, wiped them all over the tablecloth, and belched?" Mr. Ballard began warming up for another lecture. "Would you invite them back?"

"Maybe," Melissa answered, "if I liked them enough."

Mrs. Ballard shook her head. "Well, I don't think I'd like them very much."

"Have I been describing one of your friends?" Mr. Ballard joked.

Melissa wondered what table manners were like on Zironia. Did they use knives and forks and napkin rings? It hardly mattered. Solay wouldn't be coming to dinner at her house.

Melissa pushed her plate aside. "I don't want to be impolite," she said, "but I'm not very hungry tonight. Can I go upstairs and practice?"

Her parents looked at each other.

"Is everything all right?" Mrs. Ballard asked.

"Fine."

"Better for her to play her violin than with the vegetables," Mr. Ballard said. "Elena overcooked them anyway."

"Thanks," Melissa said, and left the table before her mother had a chance to argue.

Upstairs in her bedroom, she opened her violin case. But the thought of thirty minutes of scales followed by another thirty minutes of Bach made her quickly shut the case again. Too much had happened that day to concentrate on the violin. She closed the door and switched on her tape deck, putting in a cassette Mr. Hofheinz had recorded of the correct way to play some études she had been practicing. Turning the volume up loud enough for her parents to hear downstairs, she picked out another tape for herself, one she had discovered in her mother's music collection. Sitting outside on her balcony, she played *Sgt. Pepper's Lonely Hearts Club Band* softly on her Walkman. Despite Mr. Hofheinz and her father, the Beatles were much better company than Bach.

Listening to "Lucy in the Sky with Diamonds," Melissa thought about Solay. Were the Beatles imagining someone like the spacegirl when they sang about "a girl with kaleidoscope eyes"? Were there "tangerine trees and marmalade skies" on Zironia? Melissa searched the stars again to find Solay's planet, but without Solay to guide her, she wasn't sure whether she was looking in the right place. She wondered if being millions of miles away from Zironia made Solay homesick. Did she worry whether she'd ever see her parents again?

Maybe she's lonely, too, Melissa thought. Maybe I was wrong to get so angry with her.

Then she thought of the disaster with the snails and Solay's instant disappearance. And Solay had had the nerve to blame it all on her.

Melissa shuddered to think what would have happened if Mrs. Rademacher had told her parents about the snails. Bringing snails to lunch was definitely not polite. But neither was stealing lunches, she thought bitterly. If people were mean to you, why should you be nice to them? What was wrong with treating them the same way they treated you?

Sitting there in the dark, she felt a twinge of doubt

about sending Solay away. Maybe she'd been too hard on her. Shivering in the cold night air, Melissa realized that she would miss the warmth of Solay's snuggling under the covers with her at night.

9

Saturday morning, Melissa packed her bathing suit and towel and rode her bicycle the two miles to Crestwood Estates' recreation center. Sports were an important part of the "better life" of Crestwood Estates. Everyone who lived there seemed to play golf or tennis or volleyball or jog regularly or swim.

"A healthy person must be physically as well as mentally fit," pronounced Mr. Ballard, whose main physical activity was rising early three mornings a week to ride his stationary bike while he read the newspaper.

Mrs. Ballard was not very athletic either, having tried both golf and tennis without success, but she thought swimming a wonderful opportunity for Melissa. "I wish I'd taken up a sport when I was young," she claimed.

The Ballards' encouragement was actually unnecessary. On her own Melissa had discovered that she enjoyed swimming, and she looked forward to her Saturday lessons. Crestwood Estates had a strong competitive swimming program, and most of the girls in her class had been taking lessons for years. But Melissa didn't mind that they were stronger or better swimmers; in fact, she liked not being among the best. Neither the swimming teacher nor her parents expected her to be a champion. Showing up for class was enough to make them happy.

The only thing she didn't like about swimming was that Caitlin was in her class. And wherever Caitlin went, so did her shadow, Celia. They were both getting out of Caitlin's father's BMW as Melissa approached the rec center on her bike. She slowed down to avoid them.

Caitlin was too busy modeling her new denim jacket to notice. Even from a distance Melissa could see it wasn't the kind of jacket you found on the racks in department stores. It had some kind of designs stitched on the front pockets and two dolphins appliquéd on the back. Melissa thought it loud and cheesy, but Solay probably would have loved it. A few girls crowded admiringly around Caitlin.

Melissa took her time locking up her bike until Caitlin and the others had entered the women's locker room. Then she followed them inside. She found an empty locker away from the other girls and began to change.

"Is that locker taken?" Sally Gillkey timidly pointed to the open door next to Melissa's.

Melissa shrugged and hurried to put on her bathing suit. Next to Trisha Archer, who limped because of an accident that left one leg shorter than the other, Sally was the worst swimmer in the class. Although Melissa wasn't that much better, she didn't want the other girls to lump her in the same group as Sally and Trisha. She had enough problems as it was.

Sally sat down on the bench and untied her tennis shoes. "I know Caitlin lied about the snails yesterday," she said without looking up from her laces.

"So why didn't you say something?"

"I wanted to, but Mrs. Rademacher didn't give me a chance. . . ."

"Well, it's too late now." Melissa grabbed her towel and slammed the locker shut. She didn't know why Sally kept coming to swimming classes. Because Trisha was disabled, the girls were embarrassed to make fun of her when she was around, but they had no hesitation saying mean things in front of Sally. "Who swims like a walrus, stinks like one too? Smelly Sally Gillkey."

If Sally weren't in class, Melissa wondered whether they would pick on her instead.

Outside, the swim teacher, a college student named

Rosie, led them through stretching exercises to warm up. Then they all jumped into the pool. In her care to stay away from Sally and Trisha, Melissa didn't pay attention to Caitlin and Celia, and they all ended up in the same lane. To keep two swimmers to a lane, Rosie moved Celia to the next one, leaving Caitlin and Melissa together.

"Look who's here," said Caitlin, "the snail-lover."

Celia laughed from across the buoy that separated their lanes. "She swims like one."

"You mean creeps like one," said Caitlin.

Melissa felt a sharp cramping in her stomach. Why did they spoil everything? Why couldn't they leave her alone?

She took a deep breath and let herself sink to the bottom of the pool. The water muffled all the sounds of their laughter.

Melissa rose to the surface as Rosie blew her whistle to begin the lesson.

Shaking the water from her hair, she unintentionally sprayed Caitlin.

"Hey, watch that! Stay out of my face," Caitlin warned as they lined up at the end of the pool.

"And you stay out of mine," Melissa muttered, but so softly that Caitlin couldn't hear.

"What?" Caitlin said threateningly.

Rosie's whistle saved Melissa from answering. They were working on the crawl this week, and Rosie had them all swim two laps to observe their strokes.

Melissa started off slowly and evenly, careful to keep her fingers together and legs straight as Rosie had taught them. Caitlin quickly sped ahead. One of the strongest swimmers in the class, she finished almost half a lap ahead of Melissa.

"I bet even Trisha could beat you," she taunted.

Melissa's arms tensed and her chest tightened. This time she would show Caitlin.

The next two laps Rosie instructed them to focus on their breathing. But Melissa had another goal. She pushed off hard against the side of the pool and came up kicking like an eggbeater and digging her arms through the water with as much force as she could.

Her burst of speed caught Caitlin by surprise. Seeing Melissa race past, Caitlin immediately increased her pace, but Melissa still reached the end of the pool ahead of her. Caitlin had a stronger racing turn and caught up to Melissa on the return lap. Though her legs ached and her shoulders felt as if they were straining at the sockets, Melissa refused to give up. Caitlin touched the wall only an arm's length ahead of her.

"Out of breath already?" Caitlin gasped.

"No more . . . than you . . ." Melissa gulped for air.

"Hey, you two, this isn't a race," Rosie called to them. "We're working on our forms today, not pool records." To test how efficiently they were swimming, she asked them to count the number of strokes it took to get from one end of the pool to the other.

"You want to try that again?" Caitlin challenged.

"Sure," Melissa agreed, even though she knew that with Caitlin racing from the start, she had no chance to beat her.

But Caitlin wasn't taking any chances of losing. As they pushed off from the side of the pool, she grabbed the bottom of Melissa's two-piece bathing suit and yanked it partway down her leg. Panicked, Melissa groped for her suit, swallowed water, and rose to the surface spitting. By then, Caitlin was far down the pool.

Melissa was the last person in the class to finish.

"I told you Trisha was faster." Caitlin grinned.

Without thinking, Melissa struck the water with the palms of her hands, splashing Caitlin in her face. Caitlin looked as stunned as she was.

Rosie instantly blew her whistle. "You know better than that, Melissa. Out of the pool!"

Caitlin ducked her face in the water to hide her smirk.

At the other end of the pool, Sally stared in open-mouthed amazement.

Melissa's face burned as she climbed out of the water. Grabbing her towel, she headed straight for the lockers.

It wasn't fair! Yesterday, Mrs. Rademacher, today,

Rosie. How could they blame her when it was all Caitlin's fault? She kicked the locker door, banging her toe in the process. Damn! Damn! Triple damn! She couldn't even get angry without hurting herself.

"*Magi!*" exclaimed a familiar voice.

"I told you to stay away," Melissa snapped, turning to find Solay leaning on a locker at the far end of the row.

"But you didn't really mean it," Solay replied. She was wearing a clashing two-piece bathing suit; the purple top and aquamarine bottom looked like they belonged to different suits.

"That's the worst-looking bathing suit I've ever seen," Melissa said.

"You have no sense of color." Solay hopped up on the bench and pirouetted on her toes.

"I suppose you stole that from Caitlin's closet," Melissa said sourly.

"No, I took it from a big box of clothes her family was giving away. To the homeless, I think." Solay smiled. "But I thought it would look better on me."

"It looks goofy."

"You're just saying that because it's Caitlin's."

"I don't care whose it is. It's dumb." Melissa yanked her locker open.

"Oh, excuse me, I keep forgetting how smart you are. Splashing Caitlin in the pool—that was certainly a demonstration of your superior intelligence."

71

"She deserved it."

"Right! You certainly showed her. I saw how upset she was when Rosie kicked you out of the pool."

"The snails didn't work any better." Melissa stripped off her wet bathing suit.

Solay rose on her toes and slithered across the bench toward Melissa. "I have another idea," she whispered.

"Keep it to yourself!" Melissa held her towel up like a shield.

"It's guaranteed to make Caitlin angrier than a wazanazi."

"A what?"

"A wazanazi is a little animal on Zironia that runs around in circles when it gets mad."

Melissa tried to imagine Caitlin acting like that. "Whatever you're thinking, it's just going to get me into more trouble."

Solay laughed. "You're already in trouble, Miss No-Longer-Perfect."

Melissa flung the towel at her. "Keep away!" she yelled.

"Oooh, it's such a good idea," Solay tempted.

"I don't want to hear it."

"Afraid you might like it too much?"

Melissa turned her back to finish dressing. Behind her she heard Solay hop off the bench and dart away. A minute later an arm covered in blue denim emerged snakelike at the end of the row of lockers. The pale hand attached to it beckoned to Melissa.

"What are you doing?" Melissa cried.

Solay stepped out into the aisle wearing Caitlin's jacket. "I'm just trying it on for size."

"That's stealing."

"No, just borrowing."

"I won't do it!" Melissa declared flatly.

"You don't have to take it for yourself. All you have to do is misplace it so Caitlin can't find it."

"That isn't very nice." Melissa felt herself weakening.

"Caitlin's hardly nice to you. Think of how many times she's stolen your lunch," Solay reasoned. "Let her see how it feels to lose something for a change."

"Where would we hide it?" Melissa asked nervously.

"How about Sally's locker?"

Melissa imagined Caitlin's fury if she found her jacket in Sally's locker. "No, that's too mean. There must be someplace else." Then it came to her. Outside the rec center was a large Goodwill box.

"A what?"

"Goodwill collects clothes for the needy," Melissa explained.

"Perfect," said Solay, slipping off the jacket and tossing it on the bench in front of Melissa.

A mother walked past leading her young daughter to the showers. Melissa's heart began to race, and sweat broke out on her forehead. Was she really going to do this?

"Wc'd better hurry before they finish their lesson," Solay urged.

Melissa stared at the jacket. Turning it over, she examined the design sewn on the back. The dopey smiles on the dolphins reminded her of Caitlin's smirk when Rosie whistled her out of the pool.

She stuffed the jacket into her gym bag with her wet bathing suit.

"See how easy it is," Solay said approvingly.

Melissa checked the locker room again. There was no one in sight. She zipped up her gym bag and walked quickly toward the exit.

"Don't leave too soon. You'll miss all the fun," Solay said, springing to the top of the lockers and lying down to wait for Caitlin's return.

Melissa walked straight toward the large yellow Goodwill container at the edge of the parking lot. Looking around to make sure no one was watching, she dropped Caitlin's jacket through the slot in the box. It would make some poor girl happy.

Then she climbed the hill behind the rec center and sat down to watch the rest of the lesson from a safe distance. She was too far away to make out their voices, but still close enough for the class to see her if they happened to look up. From time to time, she noticed Rosie glancing in her direction. She hoped Rosie was feeling bad for kicking her out.

74

When class was over, Melissa walked down the hill toward the parking lot, taking her time about leaving. Then she heard what she was waiting for, a shriek as shrill as Rosie's whistle coming from inside the locker room.

Melissa mounted her bike with wobbly knees and tried to ride off casually.

10

"Tell me again about Caitlin's tantrum."

"I've told you already. It's boring to repeat."

Solay had returned that evening right after Melissa's parents had left for dinner and a movie. Now the two girls were eating popcorn and watching television on Mr. and Mrs. Ballard's king-size bed. Elena had come in to babysit for the evening and was downstairs watching television.

"Just once more," Melissa begged, hoping that this time Solay's account might make her feel more triumphant.

"Okay, but this is the last time," Solay said. She sat on the bed in Melissa's pink flannel nightgown tossing popcorn in the air and catching the kernels neatly on her tongue, like a frog snapping up flies. "When Caitlin opened the locker and saw her jacket was missing, she swore. She swore a lot. Then she threw all her clothes on the floor. Then she screamed. Oh, what a scream!" Even Solay seemed impressed. "Then she ran around naked, opening up everyone else's locker and flinging *their* clothes on the floor."

"You didn't say that about her being naked before."

Solay threw some more popcorn in the air and kept it suspended there with her eyes. "Maybe she had on the bottom of her bikini. I forget." She blinked and the kernels dropped into her open mouth.

"And you're making that up about her going through everyone else's locker, too, aren't you?"

Solay shrugged. "If you don't like the way I tell it, imagine it yourself."

The trouble was, no matter how Melissa imagined Caitlin's reaction, it didn't make her feel any better. "Did she say anything about me?" Melissa asked nervously.

"I didn't wait around to hear, but when she thinks about it, I'm sure your name will come up."

That was exactly what Melissa was afraid of.

"Oh, stop worrying," Solay said impatiently. "She can't prove anything. What's she going to do?"

The uncertainty made Melissa even more nervous.

"C'mon, let's have some fun." Solay threw more popcorn in the air.

Melissa tried to imitate her example but couldn't catch any of the kernels in her mouth, and they fell all over the bed.

Solay looked at her as if she were hopeless. "You're going to need months of practice," she said, tossing up another handful.

Melissa stuck her hand in front of Solay's face, scattering the popcorn everywhere.

Solay shook her head. "What a spoilsport!"

"We'd better clean up this mess," Melissa said.

Solay lifted a corner of the sheet and brushed the loose popcorn underneath the covers. "If you're going to be bad," she said, "you might as well enjoy it. Otherwise, why bother?"

All Sunday, whenever Melissa's parents weren't around, Solay coached her on how to act at school on Monday. "Caitlin's jacket stolen? Oh, *no!*" She gestured with exaggerated horror. "Who would do anything like that?"

Melissa rolled her eyes.

"Okay, show me how you'd do it."

Melissa tried out several different ways of pretending surprise in front of her dresser mirror, but each one seemed phonier than the other.

"You're right," Solay agreed. "Better not say anything. Just act the way you usually do, as if you couldn't care less about something as unimportant as Caitlin's jacket."

"No one will believe that!" Melissa protested.

"Of course they will. Why would Miss Perfect bother herself about Caitlin's jacket? You're so good, how could anyone suspect you?" Solay leaned over Melissa's shoulder and grinned wickedly at her in the mirror.

Despite Solay's coaching, by Monday morning Melissa was so nervous that her stomach felt as lumpy as the bowl of oatmeal waiting for her at the breakfast table. Just looking at it made her sick. She pushed the cereal away, wondering if it wouldn't be better to stay home this morning. But skipping school would only convince her classmates she had something to hide. She had to face them sometime.

"You're not eating your oatmeal," Mrs. Ballard noticed.

Impatient as always to get going, her father came to her rescue. "The longer she dawdles over her oatmeal, the longer I'm going to be stuck in freeway traffic. She can finish it in the car."

Carrying her backpack in one hand and her breakfast in the other, Melissa followed her father outside.

"Pssst," Solay whispered to her from the balcony, "leave the oatmeal for me."

Melissa was happy to oblige.

"And remember to look innocent," Solay reminded her.

How did someone look innocent? Inside the car Melissa lowered the front visor to check her face in the makeup mirror. Yet no matter how she arranged her mouth and eyes she looked as guilty as the criminals she saw on wanted posters in the post office.

"Why are you making those faces?" Mr. Ballard asked.

Melissa flipped up the mirror. "I'm exercising my facial muscles."

Mr. Ballard gave her a skeptical glance.

"So I don't get wrinkles," Melissa explained.

"You're ten years old."

"You can't start early enough."

Mr. Ballard looked over at her again suspiciously. "And where's your oatmeal?"

"My oatmeal?" She tried out the look of innocent surprise she had been practicing since yesterday. It didn't convince her father either.

He turned down the volume on the Bach organ fugue he was playing. "Is something bothering you, Missy?"

"No." She stared out the front window.

"You sure?" he asked again.

"We have the California State math exam today." It was all right to be nervous about exams, she thought.

"You've always been good at math. You'll do fine," he assured her.

Melissa didn't say anything more or make any more faces. Her father kept glancing at her as if he didn't believe the math test was the real problem. He didn't even turn the volume back up on the tape deck.

At the traffic light at Mimosa Boulevard, he spoke again, as if all that time he'd been thinking what to say. "In New York you used to talk to me more . . . about school, about violin lessons. . . ."

"In New York you weren't as busy."

"True, but I have time right now. If there's something on your mind . . ."

"Nothing important," she said, raising the volume on the Bach. She wasn't about to engage in a long discussion about stealing.

Mr. Ballard frowned, but he didn't press her.

Approaching the school, Melissa nervously scanned the street. Then she saw them: the three Fashion Witches, all wearing black today, dressed for her funeral no doubt. They were standing in their regular spot on the front lawn; only this morning they were surrounded by a larger group than usual.

Melissa's stomach dropped like a cannonball as the girls turned toward the Volvo.

This is all Solay's fault, she thought.

"You sure you're all right, honey?" Mr. Ballard asked as she picked up her backpack.

She nodded, her mouth too dry to speak. Stepping out of the car, she took a deep breath and started across the lawn, feeling like a blind woman walking toward the edge of a cliff.

"Hey, Melissa, where you hurrying?" Caitlin called in what appeared to be a friendly tone.

"Yeah, what's your rush? The bell hasn't even rung yet," Celia added.

Melissa warily slowed her step.

"You were in a pretty big rush to leave the pool on Saturday, too," Caitlin said.

"I got kicked out, remember?" Melissa's voice was a little shaky.

David was among the fifth graders hanging out on the front lawn. "They kicked *you* out of the pool?" he said in amazement.

"What for?" Dougie sneered. "Throwing snails in the water?"

Caitlin ignored the boys' comments. "Did you see anybody in the lockers with my jacket?"

Melissa shook her head, aware that the three Fashion Critics were studying her closely.

"You sure?" Caitlin asked again. "Because somebody stole it while I was swimming."

"Oh!" It was all Melissa could trust herself to say.

"She doesn't seem that surprised," Celia said.

"No, she doesn't," Rochelle agreed.

Caitlin stepped uncomfortably close. "The jacket was a present from my father. He had it specially made. The dolphins were his design. . . ." Her voice broke.

Melissa had expected Caitlin to be furious; she'd

82

never imagined that she might cry. "Maybe somebody will find it," she offered feebly.

"Did you report it to the police?" Dougie asked.

The police! Melissa froze.

"Not yet," Caitlin said, "but if it doesn't turn up by tomorrow, my father's going to call them."

Melissa pictured the police car pulling up to her house and the officers coming to the door to arrest her.

"Whoever stole Caitlin's jacket is pretty low," Celia said, staring directly at Melissa.

"Yeah," Rochelle echoed. "The thief better return it, or else her parents will be bringing her a Thanksgiving basket in juvenile hall."

Melissa stood there blank, wordless.

David came to her rescue. "They don't put kids in jail for stealing a jacket."

"Yeah, they could," Dougie argued. "The cops can do anything they want."

The bell rang and the students began heading toward the door.

"Caitlin's father was real upset by this," Celia warned as she walked away. "Who knows what could happen if she doesn't get her jacket back?"

David lagged behind with Melissa as the others entered the building. "You didn't really steal her jacket, did you?"

Melissa flushed with shame and anger. "It's not your problem!" she recovered her voice in a burst.

He looked at her in astonishment. "Jeez!" he whistled. "You really are in trouble."

She turned and ran in the opposite direction of the school.

Three blocks past Ralph Waldo Emerson, Melissa finally slowed to a walk to catch her breath. Except for a few gardeners mowing lawns and a woman pushing a baby stroller, the streets of Crestwood Estates were deserted. Melissa found a shady spot under a laurel tree and waited for Solay. She knew it wouldn't take long for the spacegirl to appear. Trouble attracted her like garbage attracted flies.

"That's not a very nice way of putting it," Solay chided.

Melissa turned to find her sitting astride a large, ugly sculpture of a stone fish at the entrance of an overdecorated front lawn. "Why not the way flowers attract bees?"

"How about the way crime brings policemen?" Melissa shot back.

"Get a grip," Solay said, sliding down the back of the fish. "You're just letting Caitlin bully you again. She's not going to turn you in to the cops."

"No, she isn't," Melissa declared, "because we're going back right now to get her jacket and return it."

Solay studied her a moment with her mismatched eyes. "Whatever you say." She turned and did a perfect cartwheel.

Ignoring her acrobatics, Melissa set off briskly for the rec center. Solay bounded ahead of her, cartwheeling across lawns and leaping over hedges.

When they reached the rec center, several women with tennis rackets were chatting in the parking lot near the Goodwill container. The girls hid behind a station wagon, waiting for them to leave. The women talked on endlessly.

A large yellow truck rumbled into the parking lot. Melissa's stomach dropped as she read the lettering on the truck: HELPING THE HANDICAPPED.

The truck pulled up to the Goodwill box.

"We've got to do something!" Melissa whispered.

Solay shrugged. "This was your idea."

A man got out of the cab and opened the rear door of the truck.

"Please, I need your help," Melissa begged.

"Tell him the truth, that you gave the jacket away and now you've changed your mind."

"He won't believe that."

"How do you know until you've tried?"

Melissa's hands began to sweat. Though she wanted to speak to the workman, she couldn't bring herself to step out from behind the car. What if he thought she was stealing from the poor? What if one of the tennis ladies was a friend of Caitlin's mother?

She watched, paralyzed, as the workman loaded the contents from the Goodwill box onto the truck. Among the jumble of old clothes, she spotted the dolphins on Caitlin's jacket.

"You've got to help," Melissa pleaded. "Use your magic to float the jacket over here."

"I can't steal from the handicapped," Solay said righteously.

The workman closed the back doors of the truck and got in the cab. The driver pulled away.

"Well, so much for good intentions," Solay said as the truck disappeared down the street.

Melissa kicked the tire of the station wagon. "You could've done something."

"I don't care if Caitlin gets her jacket back."

"She was practically crying at school this morning."

"Serves her right. How many times has she made you feel that way?"

Even though it was true, Melissa didn't feel any pleasure in getting even. Were lying and stealing the only ways to stand up to people like Caitlin?

"If you spoke up for yourself, you wouldn't have to

lie," Solay said as they walked away. "On Zironia no one lies because we can all read each other's thoughts."

"But it was your idea to steal Caitlin's jacket," Melissa reminded her.

"When you're on another planet, you should follow its customs." She plucked a late-blooming daisy from a front yard and casually began to pick its petals.

The gesture irritated Melissa. "If everything's so wonderful on Zironia, why did you come here?"

"I told you, it's part of my education." Solay plucked the petals faster.

"I don't think so. I think you did something really bad there. So bad they sent you away."

A burst of red flared on Solay's white cheeks. "It wasn't really that terrible. Just a little thoughtless."

"What did you do?"

"I'd rather not talk about it, if you don't mind."

Melissa tried to imagine what crime Solay could have committed to be banished millions of miles from home.

"Anyway, I'm not here forever," Solay reminded her. "I can go back anytime."

"Why don't you?"

Solay ripped the last petal from the daisy and threw it away. "I have to make a few changes first."

"No wonder you're still here," Melissa exclaimed. "You haven't changed a bit since you landed—except for wearing clothes."

"You're not making it any easier," Solay snapped.

"*Me?*" Melissa scoffed. "How can this be *my* fault?"

"Because before I can return to Zironia I have to help someone out. It's one of the lessons I have to learn—how to be a friend. And you're making it very hard," she grumbled.

"And *you're* not? Why didn't you tell me this at the beginning?"

"I didn't know yet whether I wanted to be your friend."

"Do you?" Melissa asked shyly.

"Well, you could certainly use my help."

"I'm not a charity case!"

"Then don't act like one. '*Please, I need your help,*' " Solay whined.

Now Melissa blushed.

"How can I help you if you're not ready to stand up for yourself?" Solay asked.

"I'm ready," Melissa declared softly.

Solay studied her a moment, clearly unconvinced. "We'll see."

"Try me," Melissa insisted.

"Okay. Caitlin's jacket is history, and you're almost an hour late for school. What do you do now, Miss Perfect?"

Melissa's stomach began to churn again. How was she ever going to explain this to Mrs. Rademacher? "I need to think of a good lie."

"Oh, great idea, Missy. Way to stand up for yourself," Solay hooted.

Melissa felt her cheeks go hot. "Well, what do you suggest?"

"I suggest . . ." Solay paused dramatically, "a holiday."

"A holiday?"

"Why not? As long as you've missed math, why not ditch for the whole day? If you're going to get in trouble, you might as well enjoy yourself."

"That's standing up for myself?"

"Absolutely. If you're going to get punished, you should enjoy the crime. It's called having the courage of your convictions."

Melissa hesitated. So far, every time she had listened to Solay it had been disastrous. But showing up late for school without a good excuse or Caitlin's jacket was clearly going to be a catastrophe, too. "What about Caitlin?" she asked.

"Don't worry. I'm working on that," Solay said confidently. "But it's hard to think on an empty stomach."

"We have the lunch my mother packed."

"Tuna fish again." Solay made a face. "I was thinking more like McDonald's."

"McDonald's! You've been watching TV when I'm not around," Melissa realized.

"How else can you learn about America?" Solay grabbed her hand. "C'mon, I hear they have great fries."

12

With a scarf hiding her face and Melissa's jeans and jacket covering her pale limbs, Solay blended in at the mall more easily than Melissa had imagined. No one seemed to notice her peculiarities or suspect she might be a tourist visiting from another planet.

They bought Cokes and fries at McDonald's and sat at one of the tables outside the mall's fast-food restaurants. "French fries are definitely something I'm going to bring back to Zironia," Solay said between bites.

"You can't go home until you've helped me out," Melissa reminded.

"Don't worry. I've got a new plan!" Solay scooped up more potatoes from the box they were sharing.

Melissa grabbed another handful before Solay gobbled them all up. "Are you going to tell it to me? Or make me guess?"

"It's time for you to tell the truth," Solay advised.

Melissa's stomach clenched. "You want me to tell Caitlin I stole her jacket?"

"That's not the truth I was thinking about. It's all those other things you've wanted to say but have been afraid to."

"What things?"

"You know what they are. And it's time the Fashion Critics did, too."

"You want me to tell them in person?" Melissa asked uneasily.

Solay gave her a sour look. "You said you were ready."

"What if I lose my voice? Or stutter?"

"Even if you whisper, they'll still hear it."

Melissa tried to imagine herself confronting the Fashion Critics on the lawn outside of school. The three girls all leaned forward to hear, but no words came from Melissa's mouth. "Do you have any other ideas?" she asked.

Solay considered it. "I suppose you could write down what you think. You could send notes to each of them."

"That's better." Relieved, Melissa quickly found a pen and notebook in her backpack.

"Start with Rochelle," Solay directed. "She's the easiest."

"Dear Rochelle," Melissa wrote. "Now what?"

"The truth!" Solay commanded, polishing off another fry.

Melissa thought a moment, then began to write: "You may be the prettiest girl in the class, but you're also the dumbest. Why do you let Caitlin boss you around all the time when she makes fun of you behind your back? Do you know she thinks you need a nose job?"

"Good, very good," Solay approved. "Especially the part about her nose."

"It's true, too." Melissa grinned, beginning to enjoy herself. "I heard Caitlin say it to Celia a few weeks ago in the lavatory."

"Well, it's time Rochelle heard it, too. She needs a friend who's not afraid to tell her the truth."

Next Melissa composed a note to Celia: "How come you hang around Caitlin all the time like a dog waiting for table scraps? Can't you see she only likes you because you agree with everything she says? What kind of best friend is that? Get a life."

"Cold!" Solay giggled.

"But true!" Melissa laughed.

Finally, she wrote to Caitlin. The note was easier than she expected. "You're not the smartest girl in the fifth grade, or the prettiest, or even the best-dressed (Celia is). But you are the meanest. Why? Are you scared nobody will be nice to you otherwise? The truth is they wouldn't. You're whiny and cruel and selfish.

But no one will say so because they're scared you'll pick on them. THE REAL TRUTH IS THAT NO ONE LIKES YOU."

"Now, wasn't that satisfying?" Solay asked.

Melissa had to admit it was.

"See, honesty is the best policy!"

They celebrated by spending the last of Melissa's money on a hot fudge sundae. When they'd finished, they still had almost three hours left until the end of school. "I think we should try on some clothes," Solay announced.

For the next few hours, she led Melissa from one store to another, trying on jeans, tops, sweaters, leggings, dresses, jewelry, and hats. And various combinations of each. Melissa had never realized that shopping could be so much fun. With Solay it didn't matter whether the clothes she picked out were too expensive or too impractical or too loud or even matched. She was free to sample anything she wanted in the dressing rooms. Jeans and straw hats. Cowboy boots and bonnets with veils. Leggings and leather jackets. The wilder the outfit, the more clashing the colors, the more Solay approved.

By the time they had run out of shops, the school day was almost over. "We can go home now," Melissa said, worn out by their holiday.

"Aren't you forgetting something? Don't you have some notes to deliver?"

Melissa's stomach did a backflip. "Isn't it enough to just write them?"

"You want them to keep picking on you?"

"But what if the notes make them even angrier?"

Solay snatched the letters from the pocket of Melissa's backpack. "You're much more fun when you're not worrying."

"Hey, give those back!" Melissa grabbed for the letters.

Solay danced away. "You going to stay scared of them for the rest of your life?"

Melissa chased after her. "They're my notes. I'll deliver them when I'm good and ready."

"*I'm* ready to deliver them this afternoon." Solay skipped ahead, keeping just out of Melissa's reach.

Half a block from school, they stopped and hid behind a large palm tree on the other side of the street. Melissa waited for her chance to steal the notes back.

The last bell rang, and like a radio clicking on, the school suddenly rumbled with sound. Doors sprang open. Shouts and high-pitched voices filled the air.

Melissa watched from her hiding place as students emerged in groups or pairs. Everybody seemed to have at least one friend. Bent low under his heavy backpack, David walked with Dougie, who carried no books, but dragged an old piece of rope, idly whacking the bushes in his path. The Fashion Critics sashayed across the lawn like chorus girls, in matching outfits of black tights and miniskirts. Even Sally Gillkey had a partner, Trisha Archer.

Melissa was too far away to hear any of their conversations. "Are they talking about me?" she asked Solay.

Solay narrowed her eyes and gazed across the street. "David's worried about the math test. He thinks he missed two questions and his parents will be disappointed . . . Dougie's not listening. He's looking for something to hit. . . ."

"What about Caitlin?" Melissa saw the Fashion Critics stop to say something to Trisha and Sally.

"Oh, you're right—they are talking about you! Caitlin's warning them not to be your friend. . . ."

Sally's face reddened and she shook her head.

"But Sally's saying, don't worry, you're too stuck on yourself to be anybody's friend."

Melissa saw the Fashion Critics laughing as they flounced away.

"You sure you don't want to deliver these yourself?" Solay held out the notes.

Melissa snatched them from her. What did she have to lose? They all hated her anyway. She might as well tell the truth.

"I'll be right behind you," Solay encouraged.

They crossed the street at a safe distance and circled behind the school, entering from the back. Although there were still a few people in the halls, neither Mrs. Rademacher nor any fifth graders were in sight.

With Solay at her heels, Melissa peered cautiously around the corner to check the corridor to her classroom. It was empty. Solay placed a hand at the base of Melissa's spine and shoved her forward. It took only a few seconds to plant the letters in Rochelle's and Celia's adjoining lockers. Melissa was searching for Caitlin's locker when she heard heavy footsteps padding toward the door inside Mrs. Rademacher's classroom.

There was no time to escape to the playground. All she could do was flatten herself against the side of the arts-and-crafts case and hold her breath. With her usual lightness, Solay leaped to the top of the cabinet to hide.

Mrs. Rademacher opened the door of her classroom and, without even a glance in Melissa's direction, headed the other way down the hall. Solay dropped down lightly beside Melissa as she was letting out her breath.

"Quick, before she comes back!" Solay nodded to the open door.

Unable to think for herself anymore, Melissa blindly followed Solay into the classroom and stuck the remaining letter on Caitlin's chair. Within seconds, they escaped to the playground undetected.

"I can't wait until tomorrow," Solay said as they headed home.

Melissa was just happy she hadn't signed her name.

13

The first thing Melissa did when she got home was sit down at her mother's computer to write a fake excuse to explain her absence to Mrs. Rademacher. The truth, in this case, simply wouldn't work. How could she tell either her teacher or her parents the real reasons she'd missed school?

After trying out several diseases in her mind, she finally settled on "an acute stomachache." The "acute" sounded serious enough to keep someone at home, yet a stomachache was something you could recover from in a day. She also liked "acute" because it sounded adult, a word her speechwriter mother might use. The computer made it even easier. It meant all she had to forge was her mother's signature.

She was printing out the note on her mother's sta-

tionery when her mother pulled into the driveway—
an hour earlier than usual. Melissa turned off the computer and quickly straightened up the desk. She hid
the letter in a schoolbook, then sauntered into the
kitchen, where Elena was preparing dinner.

Her mother entered looking tense and exhausted.

"You're home early," Melissa said.

"I have a splitting headache." Mrs. Ballard ran both
hands through her hair.

"Mr. Stohlmyer?"

"Who else?" She yanked open a kitchen drawer and
found the aspirin.

"Why don't you tell him to stop being so mean?"
Melissa asked.

"It isn't that easy." Mrs. Ballard swallowed two aspirin without water.

"Maybe you need to practice. You could try saying
it to me," Melissa offered.

Mrs. Ballard smiled sadly. "Thanks, honey, but
you're not the one who's being mean."

"You should write him a letter, tell him he's a cruel
old man."

For an instant Mrs. Ballard seemed to consider the
idea, but then rejected it. "I don't want to lose my
job." She gripped her head again. "I'm sorry, I have
to lie down for a while."

"Your momma work hard," Elena said as Mrs.
Ballard went upstairs to take a nap.

"Too hard," Melissa agreed. And she worried too much besides. Her mother needed Solay's help as much as she did.

Mrs. Ballard was still sleeping when Mr. Ballard returned home; so he and Melissa ate dinner without her in the kitchen. There was not much to talk about over Elena's cardboard-dry chicken. Melissa couldn't tell her father how she'd spent her day, and her father didn't want to discuss his. "Some days are better off forgetting," he said. Instead of conversation, he put on a CD of Mozart's *Jupiter* Symphony, "much stronger than aspirin for the headaches of the world."

After dinner Melissa left him with Mozart and went upstairs to her balcony to be with Solay. They wrapped themselves in a blanket and sat out on a deck chair listening to *Sgt. Pepper's Lonely Hearts Club Band*.

The night was very clear, the sky sprinkled with as many stars as there were goose pimples on Melissa's skin.

"Do you miss Zironia?" she asked.

"I find Earth very fascinating," Solay answered, staring at the heavens.

"But don't you get lonesome for your parents?"

For a second, Solay's kaleidoscope eyes seemed to glisten, but in the dark Melissa couldn't be sure.

"Everybody gets lonesome sometimes," Solay said. "Don't you?"

"A lot of times," Melissa admitted.

Solay put her arm around Melissa and drew her closer under the blanket. "That's why we all need friends," she said.

Huddled tightly together, they sang along with Ringo, "I get by with a little help from my friends," and then with Paul, "It's getting better, a little better all the time."

The next morning, Melissa awoke an hour earlier than usual, feeling as keyed up and edgy as if she hadn't slept at all. Had she made a terrible mistake in sending the notes?

"Stop worrying!" Solay ordered. "It's too late to take them back. So relax and enjoy what's going to happen."

"I'm too nervous," Melissa said.

"Well, get over it! The truth is supposed to set you free, not make you a nervous wreck."

But what if the Fashion Critics didn't react so positively to the truth?

"If you don't stop worrying, you're going to mess everything up again and be right back where you started," Solay warned.

It was one more reason for Melissa to worry.

To calm herself on the drive to school, while her father played Brahms she hummed "Getting Better" under her breath. But without the Beatles or Solay to accompany her, the music sounded thin and light.

When the car pulled up in front of Emerson, half of the fifth grade seemed to be standing on the front lawn.

"Your friends are all waiting for you, Missy," Mr. Ballard said. "Have a great day."

Melissa took a deep breath, opened the door, and marched straight toward the school entrance.

"Look who's back," Celia cried. "The book hound."

"Did you find my jacket?" Caitlin asked threateningly.

With her eyes fixed on the front door, Melissa pushed past them and entered the school. Inside, she glanced back through the scratched windowpane to see Caitlin gesturing after her.

"Now the fun begins." Solay's familiar laugh rippled through the reception area.

Melissa turned to see her hiding behind a potted palm. She raised a finger to her lips to silence her. "Stay out of sight," she hissed.

"And miss all the excitement?"

"Ssssh!"

The secretary at the front desk looked up at Melissa. "You speaking to me?" she asked.

Flustered, Melissa shook her head and hurried toward the lockers.

The bell rang and the students swarmed into the halls. Solay bounded to her favorite spot on top of the arts-and-crafts display case. Melissa took her time putting away her lunchbox, waiting to see what would happen.

David leaned over from his nearby locker. "Mrs. Rademacher asked about you yesterday."

"I bet you told her I ditched."

"No, I said you were sick."

"How come?" Melissa asked in surprise.

"I figured you were in enough trouble already," he whispered. "What did your parents say?"

"Ah . . . well . . . they don't know about it yet."

He looked at her admiringly. "I'd be too scared to do anything like that."

Behind him, she saw Rochelle color as she read the note planted in her locker. Glancing in Celia's direction, Rochelle quickly shoved the paper in her pocket.

From her perch atop the display case, Solay grinned.

The second bell rang and they all filed into class. As Melissa walked to Mrs. Rademacher's desk to deliver her excuse, she saw Celia open the note she'd found in her locker. Her face went pale as she stared at the paper. Scanning the room for the poison-penman, she discovered Rochelle glaring at her across the aisle. Celia crumpled the note and threw it her.

This was beyond even Melissa's wildest imaginings: Rochelle and Celia each thought the other had written the notes!

In the front row, Dougie coughed loudly to catch Mrs. Rademacher's attention. The teacher looked over to see Rochelle and Celia swearing at each other under their breath.

"Girls!" Mrs. Rademacher tapped her desk with her pencil. "What's going on there?"

"They're passing notes, Mrs. Rademacher," Dougie was delighted to reveal.

Mrs. Rademacher nodded for Melissa to take her seat and waddled down the aisle to confiscate the notes. "Would you like to share these with your classmates?" she asked Rochelle.

"No!" Rochelle and Celia both cried in alarm.

"Well, then please refrain from passing them in class. Notes are for keeping track of your lessons, not for exchanging gossip." She held out her hand.

Celia and Rochelle meekly placed the notes in her palm. Mrs. Rademacher put them in her pocket to examine later.

Melissa peeked over at Caitlin. Somehow the note she had left on her chair had fallen on the floor behind her.

"Now, class, let us focus our attention where it belongs," Mrs. Rademacher counseled. "Judging from yesterday's math tests, we have much to accomplish."

David raised his hand. "When will we find out our scores?"

"Soon enough," she said sternly. "This morning I'm not concerned with grades, but understanding."

David looked at her in confusion and reached in his shirt pocket for his roll of Tums.

Outside the window, Solay did a good imitation of his distress.

Melissa tried to ignore her. Maybe David wasn't as terrible as she had thought. She remembered what Solay reported him saying about the math test yesterday. It sounded like his parents expected a lot from him.

Mrs. Rademacher turned to Dougie. "Now, Douglas," she said, "please go to the board and demonstrate today's lesson."

"Me?" Dougie said in amazement.

The class snickered.

Mrs. Rademacher gave them a sharp look and handed Dougie the chalk. "Come on, Douglas, please go to the board and show the class how well you can do when you try."

"But I didn't do my homework for today," he said in embarrassment.

In the school yard, Solay mimicked Mrs. Rademacher's disapproving frown.

Melissa bit her lip to keep from laughing.

Then Solay imitated Mrs. Rademacher's rolling walk.

Despite herself, Melissa started giggling.

"What's so amusing?" the teacher demanded.

"Nothing," Melissa choked, unable to stop giggling.

Outside, Solay doubled up in laughter.

"Melissa!" Mrs. Rademacher ordered. "Get control of yourself!"

Again she bit her lip to stop, but it didn't help. All the children stared at her in astonishment. As Caitlin turned to gape with the others, she saw the note on the floor and bent to pick it up.

Mrs. Rademacher came over to Melissa's desk and put a hand on her shoulders. "Melissa, please . . ."

Her laughter quickly ended as she watched Caitlin read the note.

"This isn't true!" Caitlin exclaimed. She waved the paper in the air. "Someone's writing terrible lies, Mrs. Rademacher." She glowered at Melissa "And we all know who it is."

Even Mrs. Rademacher turned to stare at Melissa.

14

At recess, Mrs. Rademacher excused everyone but Melissa. She drew a chair up beside her gray metal desk and gestured for Melissa to sit.

To make sure Solay wouldn't make things even worse, Melissa rearranged the chair so her back was toward the windows.

Mrs. Rademacher took out the three notes she had confiscated, smoothed the wrinkled papers, and read them. Then she read them each again. "You wrote these, dear?"

Melissa didn't see any way to deny it.

"You must be very angry at these girls." In private the teacher's tone was much softer than it was in class. "Would you like to tell me why?"

Melissa thought of all the taunts, the ridicule, the stolen lunches she had suffered. "They . . . they've been mean to me" was all that she could stammer.

Mrs. Rademacher sighed. "I'm not surprised. Jealousy often makes people mean. And I know some of the children are jealous of your brightness."

Melissa stared at the floor, afraid that if she said anything she would cry.

"Unfortunately, we're all capable of meanness," Mrs. Rademacher continued. "Even you. You know these notes are cruel, don't you?"

No crueler than the way the Fashion Critics have treated me, Melissa thought.

"That's why you didn't sign them, isn't it?" Mrs. Rademacher asked. "Stooping to their meanness only makes you smaller, dear."

As small as she felt already, Melissa wished she could shrink even more, enough to escape under the crack below the door.

"Well, what are we going to do about all this?" Mrs. Rademacher asked.

"I promise it won't happen again," Melissa said earnestly.

"I appreciate that, Melissa, but promises about tomorrow don't always make up for the damages of today. Don't you think you owe these girls an apology?"

"An apology?" Melissa said weakly.

Mrs. Rademacher picked up the letter to Caitlin and read. " 'You're whiny and cruel and selfish. . . .' "

108

She peered gravely over her glasses at Melissa.

But it's the truth, Melissa thought. Why should I apologize for the truth?

"As long as these angry words remain between you and Caitlin, how can you ever expect to be friends?"

But I don't want to be friends, I just want her to stop picking on me, Melissa burned to say. Instead, she hung her head.

"Well, Melissa?" Mrs. Rademacher waited.

"Couldn't I just write her a note? You know, a note for a note?"

"Melissa!" Mrs. Rademacher frowned. "Is this the same young lady who wrote so compassionately about the homeless? What happened to your generosity of spirit? Don't Caitlin and Rochelle and Celia deserve the same consideration? I'm sure your parents would think so."

Please, oh please, don't call them, Melissa prayed.

"I wonder what they would think about this," Mrs. Rademacher persisted.

Melissa felt a sharp pain in her side, yesterday's imaginary stomachache arriving for real today. "I need to go to the bathroom," she said.

Mrs. Rademacher eyed her with suspicion. Despite Melissa's grimaces, Mrs. Rademacher was not going to let a mere stomachache deter her. "All right," she said, "but don't be long. I'll call the girls in from the playground."

Melissa rushed to the lavatory and leaned against a

sink. A second grader washing her hands at the next basin looked at her with concern. Glancing in the mirror, Melissa saw that she really did look sick. Her face was pale and her forehead beaded with perspiration. The second grader left, and Melissa ran cold water to wash her face. In the mirror, she saw Solay sitting cross-legged on the sill of one of the bathroom's frosted windows.

"Washing up to apologize?" Solay mocked.

Melissa turned on her. "I should *never* have listened to you."

"That's right, blame it all on me. Wicked Solay. The evil creature from an alien planet." She scrunched her face into a fiendish expression.

"It's not funny!"

"Oh, sorry," Solay tried to look contrite. "That was very rude, wasn't it? How could we ever stay friends?"

"You're not my friend. All you do is get me into trouble."

"No, *you're* the one who gets yourself into trouble. You let Mrs. Rademacher boss you around as much as Caitlin."

"She's my teacher!"

"Does that mean she's always right?"

"What else can I do?"

"You can argue, kick, scream, fight, throw the biggest tantrum ever seen in the fifth grade."

"I can't do that," Melissa said despairingly.

"If you give in now, the Fashion Critics will never stop picking on you," Solay warned.

Melissa felt her stomach cramp again. "What good is fighting back if you don't win?"

"Saying, 'I'm sorry' to please your teacher is hardly fighting back."

Melissa heard footsteps approaching from outside the bathroom and retreated to a stall. Solay dropped from the windowsill and followed her inside. Melissa shut the door.

"You're right," she whispered. "I can't apologize." Even the prospect of it made her stomach heave.

"Then tell them what you really feel," Solay suggested. "Right to their face. That'll show them."

"I don't know if I can."

"It's easy. Just think how sickening they are."

"They are sickening."

"Sickening as snails without their shells," Solay encouraged.

"Worse. Gross as snot."

"Gross as Dougie's boogers."

"Mean as fire-breathing monsters."

"As cold as the dark side of Urzu.

"As poisonous as toxic waste."

"You hate them."

"I hate them," Melissa said, her voice rising.

"They should all be swallowed up by a black hole."

"Mrs. Rademacher, too."

111

"She has no right to make you apologize."

"No right at all."

"She's cruel and fat," Solay declared.

"A tub of lard."

"All of them make you want to puke."

"Buckets."

"Barrels."

"Swimming pools full."

"Enough to drown them."

"Enough to drown them," Melissa repeated.

"Go on. Tell them!" Solay cheered.

Melissa opened the door to the stall.

Mrs. Rademacher stood there like a pale white balloon about to burst. Melissa didn't know how long she'd been in the lavatory, how much she'd overheard.

A wave of nausea, as powerful as an ocean swell, swept over Melissa.

Mrs. Rademacher had the presence of mind to step back a second before Melissa vomited all over her shiny black shoes.

15

Melissa lay on the cot in the nurse's office watching Miss Thorson dial her father at the university. Resting against the nurse's desk lamp was the sealed letter Mrs. Rademacher had asked the nurse to deliver to whichever of Melissa's parents picked her up.

Miss Thorson reached Mr. Ballard in his office and explained that Melissa was sick and needed to go home. Melissa could imagine his irritation on the other end of the line. Driving back to Emerson for her would disrupt his whole day.

The nurse held out the phone to Melissa. "He wants to speak to you."

"I'm sorry you're sick, honey, but I can't come for you right now," Mr. Ballard said. "I have my undergraduate lecture class in fifteen minutes. You'd better try your mom. Even though it's farther for her, she should be able to get there sooner. I couldn't pick you up until one."

Miss Thorson took the phone back and called Melissa's mother. Although it required some persuasion, she finally convinced the secretary to pull Mrs. Ballard out of the meeting she was attending. Melissa suspected it was with Mr. Stohlmyer.

It took a minute before Mrs. Ballard came to the phone. After explaining Melissa's situation once more, the nurse again handed the receiver to Melissa.

"It sounds like you have the flu," Mrs. Ballard said. "We need to get you right home to bed. The trouble is, I'm in the middle of an important meeting, and I have appointments lined up all day." She thought a second. "The best thing is for you to take a cab home. Elena can look after you until your dad or I get there. You hop into bed and rest, and I'll try to be home as soon as I can. Okay?"

Melissa returned the phone to the nurse to work out the arrangements with her mother.

It was probably just as well her parents couldn't pick her up now, she thought. They had enough to worry about at work without adding Mrs. Rademacher's letter. Better for them to open it later and only ruin their evening.

"It must be hard having parents who are so busy," Miss Thorson said when she'd hung up.

"Oh, we have a housekeeper," Melissa said, not wanting the nurse to feel sorry for her.

Miss Thorson came over to the cot and brushed Melissa's hair back gently from her forehead. "You just lie down until the cab comes," she said. "I'll take care of everything."

Melissa turned her face to the pillow to make sure she didn't cry.

Elena was waiting at the door to pay the driver when the cab pulled up to Melissa's house. "You do not feel good?" she said sympathetically as they walked inside.

Melissa shook her head. Although her cramps had disappeared, she felt lower and more discouraged than she had since the day they left New York.

Elena gave her two aspirin and sent her up to her room to sleep.

Melissa closed the door and threw herself on the bed, waiting for Solay to appear. Predictably, the spacegirl had vanished the instant Melissa had barfed on Mrs. Rademacher.

Melissa softly called her name. There was no answer.

She got up and checked the closet. Then the balcony.

Then the eucalyptus tree in the backyard. Solay wasn't in any of her favorite places.

Melissa felt a growing irritation. Whenever disaster struck, Solay immediately disappeared.

"C'mon, where are you?" Melissa called impatiently.

She opened the door to the hall and listened. The only sounds were the voices from the TV program Elena was watching in the kitchen.

Melissa checked the rest of the upstairs. "Stop playing games and show yourself!" she ordered.

Still no answer from Solay.

Melissa slammed the door of her bedroom and removed Mrs. Rademacher's letter from her backpack. Solay, she knew, would urge her to steam the envelope open. "On Zironia we have no secrets," she'd say. "Everybody knows what everyone else is thinking."

Well, it didn't take a Zironian to know what Mrs. Rademacher had written. Melissa could imagine how her parents would react. A special letter from Mrs. Rademacher! Her mother would eagerly tear it open to see what new praises Melissa had earned. What a cruel surprise! Her mother would brush her hair back nervously from her face and hand the letter to Melissa's father. He would frown and rub his beard in silence. Their daughter a liar, a forger, a thief. What would they do? Would they take her out of school? Send her to a doctor? Or, like Mrs. Rademacher in the lavatory, just stare at her in horror, as if she were some monster from another planet?

Where was Solay? How could she claim to be a friend when she ran off the moment there was real trouble?

"I resent that. I have not run off," a muffled voice spoke from underneath Melissa's bed.

Melissa dropped to her knees and lifted up the dust ruffle. Solay's clashing eyes stared out at her. "What are you doing down there?" Melissa demanded.

"Taking a nap."

"You are not. You're hiding."

"Why should I hide?" Solay backed out the other side, careful to keep the bed between them.

"Because you took off and left me to take the blame."

"It didn't seem the best time to meet Mrs. Rademacher. She was too busy cleaning off her shoes."

"It isn't funny," Melissa raged. "Every time you mess up, you run off and leave me to take the punishment. I bet you did that on Zironia, too. . . ."

"Did not."

"Then how come you're always disappearing? You tell me to stand up to Caitlin, yet you're such a coward you can't even face me."

"I'm facing you now."

"You're standing there, but you're not telling me the truth. If the truth is so important on Zironia, how come you won't tell me why you were sent here?"

Solay shifted uncomfortably on the other side of the bed. "I told you before, it's part of my education."

"I don't believe it. I think you did something so terrible your parents had to send you away. Or maybe you were just so bad they stopped loving you."

"That's not true," Solay said so softly that Melissa almost didn't hear.

"If they really loved you, they'd never send you away."

"They did it *because* they loved me." Solay turned her head and dabbed at her eyes with her slender white fingers.

"But why?" Melissa couldn't understand it. "Why would any parents do something like that?"

"Because . . . because I was too critical . . . too impatient . . . too angry. My parents wanted me to be more generous, more forgiving. . . ." Solay's eyes filled with tears. "They said I had to learn to cry."

Melissa watched in astonishment as the tears spilled down Solay's milky skin. "But didn't you ever cry on Zironia?"

Solay shook her head. "Earth is a much sadder place than Zironia," she sobbed.

"I guess it must be," Melissa said, feeling tears well up in her own eyes. Reaching across the bed, she took Solay's cold hand. They climbed on the bed and hugged each other.

"Maybe this is what friends are really for—to cry with," Melissa said.

Solay's eyes gleamed like sparks of sunlight on water. "You mean this is what my parents meant?"

Melissa nodded. "You are my best friend."

"And you're mine."

They held each other for another moment, until finally Melissa had to pull away and wipe her eyes with the corner of the bedspread. "What are we going to do now?" she asked.

"Some problems are just too hard for children," Solay admitted. "We need help."

"Where are we going to get it?"

"I'm going to try to contact my parents."

"But they're millions of miles away."

"They promised to return when I learned the lessons I was supposed to."

For the first time that afternoon Melissa felt a flash of hope. "How do we contact them?"

Solay shut her eyes and began chanting softly in Zironian. Her words rustled softly through the room like the wind rustling the eucalyptus tree outside.

16

A little before dusk, Melissa and Solay climbed the hill where they'd first met. The November wind whisked through the dry grass and crept inside Melissa's light jacket. She shivered with cold and with the fear she'd begun to feel as soon as Solay decided to contact her parents.

Would they really come? Would they be able to solve her problems? Solay, who was always confident—even when she was wrong—would not make any predictions about her parents' arrival. "Who knows where they are right now? They might be flying over China or traveling in another galaxy. It could take a few minutes for them to get here, or a few years."

Melissa figured they had, at most, an hour and a

half before her own parents returned. Her mother and father had both telephoned earlier to check her condition, but she had assured them that she was feeling better and that they needn't rush home.

Although Solay had been sending out messages all afternoon without receiving any replies, she wasn't giving up. "Thoughts, like radio waves, travel farther at night," she said as they approached the oak tree near where she had first landed. The oak was the highest point in Crestwood Estates and the perfect spot for Solay to beam her thought waves to the universe.

Melissa had brought a flashlight to help signal the spaceship if it arrived, and in her jacket pocket she carried Mrs. Rademacher's unopened letter just in case Solay's parents needed to see it. She tried to imagine what they were like. Were they completely different from the Ballards?

Solay and Melissa settled themselves underneath the oak tree. Dark rain clouds swept over the distant hills, blotting out the setting sun and turning the sky black and menacing. There were no signs anywhere of an approaching spaceship.

Solay chanted softly to herself, scanning the sky in the fading light.

"Do you see anything?" Melissa asked.

Solay shook her head.

"Can I do anything to help?"

"Sit closer. It's cold up here."

Melissa huddled closer to Solay, who had only Melissa's light, red sweater to warm her.

"*Sori, sori, Mesori, Melori . . .*" Solay chanted in Zironian in the same slow, steady rhythm as her breathing. The wind caught her reedy voice and carried it upward like a kite.

"*Mesori, Melori, hamana torgama . . .*"

Mother and Father, please come back for me.

Though the words were Zironian, Melissa understood. She and Solay had become so close that she could now read her friend's thoughts—even in another language.

"*Mesori, Melori, comprano redondo,*" Solay's voice rose above the wind.

Mother and Father, I have learned my lessons.

Melissa tightened her arm around Solay's waist. If she had learned all her lessons, she was free to return to Zironia. But Melissa didn't want her to leave yet. "It's too soon," she protested. "Way too soon."

Solay didn't answer. She rose abruptly. "Do you hear that?" she said excitedly.

Melissa could hear nothing but the wind rustling the leaves around them.

"Over there!" Solay pointed.

The sun had set behind the hills, leaving a crimson glow around them. The rest of the sky was dark with clouds.

"There, above the tree," Solay guided her.

As Melissa looked up, a beam of light split the clouds and shone down on her. She raised her arm to shield her eyes.

"*Mesori, Melori!*" Solay cried.

Solay's parents had heard her call.

The brightness was so blinding that Melissa couldn't look at it directly. Squinting from behind her arm, she glimpsed the oval outline of a spaceship.

The spacecraft didn't land but remained hovering a few feet above the oak tree. A door opened like a ramp, and two silhouetted figures emerged. They appeared to be dressed in the same kind of space suits Solay had worn on her arrival.

Solay's eyes glistened as she looked up at them. "*I knew you would come,*" she spoke to them softly in Zironian.

Her parents replied only with their thoughts.

"What are they saying?" Melissa asked nervously.

"They're very proud of me."

Melissa's chest tightened. "Have you learned every-thing you were supposed to?"

Solay nodded gravely.

"But you can't go yet. You haven't finished helping me out."

Solay looked up to her parents, then back to Melissa. "They say it's time to return now. They've missed me very much."

"It's not fair," Melissa objected. "You called

them here to help me, not to take you home."

"You won't get into nearly as much trouble without me."

"But I'm in trouble *now*. What about Mrs. Rademacher's letter?" She pulled it out of her pocket. "Ask your parents what I should do about this." She waved the letter at the spaceship.

Solay looked up at her parents for a moment, then back at Melissa. "My father says you already know what to do."

"I don't. I really don't," Melissa pleaded.

"You're the smartest girl in the fifth grade," Solay reminded her.

"They don't teach this subject in school," Melissa argued.

A ropelike ladder was lowered from the spaceship.

"Don't go!" Melissa pleaded again. "Who will I cry with when you're gone?"

Solay touched her cool forehead to Melissa's. "Think of me, and your tears will reach Zironia." She grabbed the ladder and jumped onto the bottom rung.

"What about you? How will I hear from you?"

"I will always remember you," Solay said. She turned and started up the ladder.

"Wait!" Melissa called after her. "You're wearing my favorite sweater."

Solay stopped and began to remove the red sweater.

"No, don't," Melissa called. "Keep it. It looks better on you anyway."

"Thanks, but you forget, we don't need clothes on Zironia." She dropped the sweater into Melissa's hands and quickly climbed the ladder. At the door of the spaceship, her parents embraced her. Then her father drew up the ladder.

Melissa watched from below, still squinting at the intense light. The three of them waved good-bye as the door of the spacecraft slid closed.

There was a whoosh of leaves and the beam of light pulled away, quickly shrinking to a point as tiny as a star. Then that, too, disappeared among the clouds.

Melissa slumped down beside the tree, buried her face in the sweater, and began to cry.

She was still crying when her father found her by the tree.

"What's wrong, Missy?" he asked as he knelt beside her.

She reached into her pocket and handed him Mrs. Rademacher's letter.

He put the letter into his pocket and gently pulled his daughter to her feet. With his arm around her, he led her down the hill.

17

When they reached the house and Melissa saw her mother's stricken face, she started crying all over again. Mrs. Ballard took her in her arms, and stroked her hair, and held her until her sobbing stopped. Then she sent her upstairs to bathe. Melissa lay in the warm water wondering what it would feel like to be streaking through the darkness of outer space. But she was too tired and too drained from crying to imagine anything clearly.

She changed into her nightgown and climbed into bed. Her parents joined her in her bedroom, bringing her dinner on a silver tray. Mrs. Ballard sat at the foot of the bed and Mr. Ballard in the armchair. Melissa sipped her chicken noodle soup and munched her cinnamon toast, waiting for them to speak.

"It seems that we've been very blind," Mrs. Ballard said at last.

"What did Mrs. Rademacher say?" Melissa asked.

Mr. Ballard took the letter out of the back pocket of his pants and handed it to her. Melissa unfolded the blue stationery and read the brief handwritten note.

> Dear Mr. and Mrs. Ballard,
> Please call me about Melissa. Something seems to be upsetting her at school. I'd like to be able to help, but I'm not sure exactly what the trouble is.
>
> Sincerely,
> Alice Rademacher

It occurred to Melissa that she had made a great mistake. If she had steamed the letter open when she got home, she wouldn't have panicked and Solay wouldn't have needed to call her parents for advice. And she'd still have a friend in California.

Melissa returned the letter to her father.

"Whatever's bothering you, we'd like to be able to help, too," he said. "But you have to let us know what's going on."

Melissa hesitated. How much could she really tell them?

127

"You can't go on lying forever," a voice said.

Melissa looked out to the balcony to see if Solay's face were pressed against the glass doors. But there was no one outside on the deck and no one besides her parents in the room.

The voice she'd heard had been her own.

She realized that Solay's parents had been right. She did know what to do. If she were going to start speaking up, she might as well begin at home.

"I hate Ralph Waldo Emerson," she blurted out, "and I hate Crestwood Estates." She took a breath. "And nobody at school likes me."

"Well!" Mr. Ballard said quietly.

"And I'm sick of playing the violin, too," she added.

"Ouch," he winced.

"That's a lot of hates," said Mrs. Ballard.

Mr. Ballard rubbed his beard and looked at his wife for help. "Is everything at school bad?" she asked. "What about that friend of yours, the one whose lunch they kept stealing?"

"That was me," Melissa confessed.

"Oh, sweetie," her mother said. "No wonder you're having stomachaches."

"And I stole Caitlin's new jacket, too," she divulged the worst of her sins. "Well, not really stole, but gave it away to Goodwill. . . ."

"My goodness . . ." Mr. Ballard rubbed his beard again. "We had no idea."

"You must have been very angry at Caitlin," Mrs. Ballard said.

"I hate her! I hate all of them!" Melissa railed. "I wish we'd never moved to California."

"Sometimes I wish that, too," Mrs. Ballard agreed.

Mr. Ballard looked at her in surprise. "Remember, this wasn't just my decision," he said, not wanting to take all the blame. "We decided this as a family. We thought it would be a good opportunity for all of us."

"But it hasn't been," Melissa said.

"No, it hasn't worked out exactly the way we thought," he admitted.

"So why can't we move back to New York?"

Mr. Ballard leaned forward in the chair and clasped his hands. "It's not that easy, Missy."

"Why not?"

"You can't just pick up and move across the country when things don't work out. We have to give this more of a chance."

"But Mom gets headaches working for Mr. Stohl-myer and you get heartburn being chairman," Melissa argued.

"And all this time I thought it was Elena's cooking," he tried to joke.

Mrs. Ballard gave him a sharp look. "Denying that we have problems doesn't make them any easier. Melissa's right. Look at us: headaches, stomachaches, heartburn. We're all having trouble adjusting."

Mr. Ballard sighed in acknowledgment. "I never suspected you were so unhappy, Missy," he said. "Why didn't you tell us before?"

Melissa stared at the tray. "I didn't think you wanted to hear."

Mr. Ballard got up and sat next to her on the bed. He took her hand. "Maybe we didn't," he said. "If we admitted that you had problems, maybe we'd have to look more closely at our own."

Mrs. Ballard reached over and squeezed Melissa's other hand. "I'm sorry that we've made it so hard for you to talk to us."

"So am I," Mr. Ballard said. "You should always be able to come to us with your problems. We may not always have the answer, but we can try to work out a solution together. Something better than stealing. Okay?"

"Okay," Melissa mumbled.

"If Caitlin's giving you a hard time at school, I'll be happy to talk to her parents," he offered.

Magi, Melissa thought. Her father would make even a worse mess of it than Solay.

"We won't do anything unless you want us to," Mrs. Ballard assured her. "Tomorrow I will call Mrs. Rademacher, though, and tell her that we've talked. Is there anything else you want me to say?"

"Just that I'm sorry about the shoes."

"What?" Mrs. Ballard looked puzzled.

Melissa didn't have the energy to explain. "Nothing," she said, pushing the silver tray away. "I'm very tired. I need to go to sleep."

Her father tucked her in as if she were a three-year-old, and her parents kissed her good-night and left the room. "Oh, my!" she heard her father sighing in the hall. Yet, despite her parents' surprise, they had not reacted as badly as she had expected. Even to the stealing.

She gazed out at the stars beyond her balcony and imagined Solay's spaceship speeding through the galaxy. If her thoughts could possibly catch up with her, it would take light-years for Solay to reply.

Without her, the bed felt large and empty. Melissa stretched her arms and legs out as wide as she could under the sheets to fill up all the spaces Solay had once occupied.

Melissa awoke the next morning to discover that her mother had taken the day off from work. "I have some shopping to do," Mrs. Ballard explained. "Would you like to keep me company?"

Melissa was happy to oblige.

In the car, Mrs. Ballard headed for downtown rather than the mall where they usually shopped. "Where are we going?" Melissa asked.

"On a goodwill errand."

Melissa felt her heart begin to race as she realized

where her mother was taking her. "Do you think the jacket'll still be there?"

"We can only look," Mrs. Ballard replied.

The Goodwill center was a large, corner storefront in a run-down section of the city. There were racks and tables of clothing to hunt through. After twenty minutes of searching, Melissa was ready to admit defeat. Someone had found the jacket before them.

Her hopes dashed, Melissa felt worse about the jacket than she had before. If only Solay had been willing to use her magic powers to retrieve it when they had gone back for it the first time.

Having come this far, though, Mrs. Ballard wasn't ready to give up. She sought out the store manager. Five minutes later she returned, proudly carrying Caitlin's jacket. "We're lucky." She beamed. "They hadn't priced it yet. If they'd put it on the racks, someone probably would've snatched it right away."

Melissa's pleasure at recovering the jacket was immediately dampened by the question of how she was going to return it to Caitlin. She couldn't just go up and hand it to her.

Apparently her mother was thinking the same thing. "I wonder if I shouldn't just turn this in to the lost-and-found at the pool," she suggested.

"That's a great idea," Melissa said with relief.

Afterward, they shopped for birthday presents for Melissa's father and then went out to lunch. Mrs. Ballard didn't say another word about Caitlin or school or Mrs. Rademacher. "This was fun," she said as they were finishing up their ice-cream sundaes. "You'll have to get sick more often."

"Why do I have to be sick for us to do this?" Melissa spoke without thinking.

Mrs. Ballard's spoon stopped halfway to her mouth. Her gray eyes looked sad as she put the spoon back in her dish. "You're right," she said. "We shouldn't have to fake sick days to do this."

Melissa stared at her ice cream, unable to look at her mother. She had ruined their afternoon.

After a moment she felt her mother's hand on hers. "What you said is true, even if it does hurt," Mrs. Ballard said gently.

Melissa glanced up at her mother, who was leaning across the table, gazing at her with softened eyes. "You know, you're a pretty special kid," Mrs. Ballard said.

Melissa squirmed and tried to pull her hand away. "You're just saying that because you're my mother."

"Mothers can be right, too."

"My ice cream's melting."

"So let it melt." Mrs. Ballard laughed, refusing to release her hand.

Seeing her mother's mischievous grin, Melissa realized that she'd been wrong. Her mother did know how to have fun after all. She was just out of practice.

That next morning when she awoke, Melissa decided to return to school. Although she still had no idea what she was going to do about the Fashion Critics, the prospect of facing them again no longer made her stomach churn. What worse thing could happen to her than already had?

Driving to school with her father, she felt a strange mixture of anticipation and calm. The truth was that she was curious how her class would react to her return. What did they think of her throwing up on Mrs. Rademacher?

Mr. Ballard was more nervous than Melissa. The Brahms he'd put on to calm himself seemed to have little effect. He kept looking over at Melissa to see how she was doing.

She sat in the front seat and tried to ignore his worried glances. Finally she tugged his sleeve. "Listen to the music," she said. "I'll be fine."

"You may be fine, Missy, but I'm not," he said, snapping off the tape deck. "I've been stewing about this for the last couple of days, and I'm very angry. Angry at all your silly classmates for not seeing how terrific you are. And angry at Mrs. Rademacher for not doing something about it. But, most of all, I'm angry at myself for not recognizing all this earlier. I'm really furious about that."

Melissa didn't know what to say. She couldn't remember when she'd seen her father this upset before.

"If Mrs. Rademacher isn't going to stand up for you,

I want to," he went on. "When we get to school, I'm going to give Caitlin and her friends a little talking-to."

"I don't think that's such a good idea," Melissa said quickly.

"Why not?" Mr. Ballard looked disappointed. "The only thing that bullies understand is fear. They need to know they can't pick on you without consequences."

Melissa tried to imagine her mild-mannered father lecturing the Fashion Critics about the consequences of their behavior. She doubted that he would strike much fear into their hearts.

"Thanks, Dad," she said, "but I need to handle this myself."

"Whatever you say, Missy," he reluctantly agreed, "though I'd really love to give them a piece of my mind."

They pulled up in front of the school. The usual crowd of fifth graders was gathered on the front lawn. The Fashion Critics all turned their heads at the arrival of the Volvo.

"You sure you don't want me to come with you?" he asked again.

"I'm sure," she said, opening the door before she changed her mind. If she didn't move quickly, she knew she'd lose her courage.

Grabbing her backpack, she started across the yard. The act of moving calmed her and she looked up to face her hecklers. They were lined up like vultures waiting to feed.

Caitlin's mean mouth was outlined in lipstick today. "Well, look who's back. You recovered enough to apologize?"

Melissa stopped in front of the group. "If you want to apologize, that's fine, but I don't care to."

There were a few snickers from the crowd.

Caitlin reddened. "Your sickness must have scrambled your brains. You're the one who's supposed to apologize to me."

"And me," Celia echoed.

"And me, too," Rochelle put in.

Melissa looked at the three of them, in their identical stone-washed jeans, all trying to look older today, with lipstick and a hint of blush. She didn't know why they had mattered to her so much.

"So?" Caitlin said threateningly. "So what do you have to say?"

Just behind the Fashion Critics, David, Dougie, and Sally all waited for her response.

And suddenly Melissa knew how to answer. She lay her backpack on the ground. "It's a beautiful day today, isn't it?"

And then she did a cartwheel. Not a very graceful one, but a cartwheel just the same.

"Hey, what are you doing?" Caitlin cried.

"That wasn't so hot, was it?" Melissa admitted.

She brushed off her jeans and did another one. The sky spun dizzily above her. Lying on the grass, she saw the Fashion Critics whirling in confusion.

David stepped out from behind them and extended a hand to help her up.

"Put your hands a little closer together," he advised.

"Hey, what are you doing, grade-grubber?" Caitlin pushed him aside.

David ignored her. "Like this," he said to Melissa and did an almost perfect cartwheel to demonstrate.

"Wow!" Melissa admired.

Caitlin stepped between them. "Stop!" she ordered.

"Why?" David asked. "Can't you do a cartwheel?"

"Yeah!" Dougie piped up. "Let's see you try."

"C'mon, we'll show you how," Melissa said. "If we can do one, anyone can."

"But who wants to?" Caitlin sneered.

"Yeah, that's kid stuff," Celia echoed, puffing herself up to look more grown-up.

"I know," Melissa said happily, throwing her hands out and tumbling through the air, as free and weightless as a traveler floating through the universe.